Musings

Daniel L. Walsch has been part of the communication field for more than forty years as journalist, public relations professional, press secretary, speech writer, instructor and author. His most recent books include *A Strategic Communication Approach to Crisis Situations: A Case Study Analysis of Transformative Events at George Mason University and Northern Illinois University*, published in 2011 by Lambert Academic Publishing, and *Communication Wars: Our Internal Perpetual Conflict* and *Organizational Spokesmanship: So You Want to Become a Press Secretary*, published in 2013 and 2014 respectfully by Cognella, Inc. Also, he maintains a blog, "Why Communication Matters", which may be accessed at www.myskeets.blogspot.com. He is an accredited public relations professional as certified by the Public Relations Society of America. He earned his PhD in communication at George Mason University. Dr. Walsch resides with his wife in Fairfax, VA.

Daniel Walsch

Musings

Olympia Publishers
London

www.olympiapublishers.com
OLYMPIA PAPERBACK EDITION

Copyright © Daniel Walsch 2016

The right of Daniel Walsch to be identified as author of
this work has been asserted in accordance with sections 77 and 78 of the
Copyright, Designs and Patents Act 1988.

All Rights Reserved

No reproduction, copy or transmission of this publication
may be made without written permission.
No paragraph of this publication may be reproduced,
copied or transmitted save with the written permission of the publisher, or in
accordance with the provisions
of the Copyright Act 1956 (as amended).

Any person who commits any unauthorised act in relation to
this publication may be liable to criminal
prosecution and civil claims for damage.

A CIP catalogue record for this title is
available from the British Library.

ISBN: 978-1-84897-719-8

(Olympia Publishers is part of Ashwell Publishing Ltd)

This is a work of fiction.
Names, characters, places and incidents originate from the writer's imagination.
Any resemblance to actual persons, living or dead, is purely coincidental.

First published *in 2016*

Olympia Publishers
60 Cannon Street
London
EC4N 6NP

Printed in Great Britain

Dedication

I dedicate this to Dr George J. Krein, Jr., my cousin by birth and brother by choice. Thank you for a lifetime of joy and love. You make my day every day.

Acknowledgements

There are few things better in life than having a selfless partner by one's side. I have this in my wife, Jo. Thank you for taking the time to review this silly text and give me your edits and feedback. Did you make a difference? You bet. And in all ways that were and are good. Any weaknesses in this book are because of me and my limitations that fall under the heading of "life".

Table of Contents

BY WAY OF INTRODUCTION - A FEW WORDS ABOUT ME	13
PROTOCOL	22
A CAT STORY	32
QUESTIONS	39
DARK SIDE/BRIGHT DAYS	62
IN DEFENSE OF YODELING	72
ANOTHER CAT STORY	75
LIFE OF TIE	78
MARRYING JESUS	86
THE JOY OF TWITTER	91
WHAT COULD GO WRONG?	94
EVER-GROWING GRUMPINESS	104
THEODORE ROOSEVELT, LIBRARIAN	110
UNSUNG HEROES	124
TEACHING	133

UNDER MY SKIN	**142**
NEVER DO THIS	**150**
ONE MORE CAT STORY	**153**
A FEW QUICK SHOUT OUTS	**158**
THE JOY OF COMMUNICATING	**162**

By Way of Introduction - A Few Words About Me

For nearly forty years I have worked at a higher education institution. A couple of community colleges. A couple of universities. During these many years I have experienced ups and downs as anyone would. Fortunately, I have never been convicted of a crime, nor have I ever done anything that led my co-workers to carry me up to the roof of the office building and throw me over the side. (If that ever did happen, I am saying right now I would take the rest of the day off.) Overall, it has been good and given me much satisfaction as education, despite its rising costs, is without question a good thing. However, being in higher education was not part of any master plan on my part. In fact, when it comes to planning, for most of my so-called professional life I have been much like a zombie: I live in the moment. For instance, I am sure if a zombie ever found itself in a job interview and was asked the inevitable question: "Where do you see yourself in five years?" this "living dead" creature would be stumped. If nothing else, the zombie would no doubt need a few minutes to come up with a good answer. Or any answer for that matter.

The zombie would probably scratch its chin and look up at the ceiling as we all do when asked a question we do not know the answer to. (Looking up at the ceiling, by the way, is a great way to look as if you are formulating a deep answer. The problem, of course, is when you speak and immediately reveal a response that is the opposite of something deep or thoughtful.) My guess is the best the zombie could come up with is, "Gee, I'm not sure. So long as I would be in a position where I could help people, then that is all that would matter." (Of course, knowing zombies as we all do, we know full well the zombie is really thinking "... long as I would be in a position where I could eat people...") Zombies may not be planners, but they are not idiots either. They would know enough to use the word "help" rather than "eat". Let us be realistic here, there are few things that turn off a search committee more than being told by an applicant that he or she wants to chow-down on all of them. Even zombies know that, I'm sure.

My point is, I did not accept my first job in higher education with the idea that this is where I would be spending the remainder of my professional life carrying out various administrative and instructional responsibilities. All these years later it just seems to have worked out that way. Actually, there was a small stretch during the past four decades – about six months – where I worked outside higher education. I was the public relations director for an international patent searching company owned by a native of England. Looking back, that was not the most exciting position. In fact, one of the many do-overs in my life would be taking that job. The big boss did not cotton to me all that much. ("You do know England is part of the British Isles!" is one of the many factoids he tossed my way in one of his moments of exasperation with me.) Fortunately, there were not too many of those moments – at least from my perspective – as my time with that company did not last long. The company suffered some unexpected financial setbacks and, as a result, I was discharged as quickly as I was hired. Good-bye paycheck. Hello unemployment.

Being without a job for several months was not the worst thing that ever happened to me. The worst thing was probably getting stuck in New York City's Lincoln Tunnel for nearly three hours and having to go to the bathroom, yet not being able to. It was awful. Holding it in for that long was absolute torture. But hold out I did. Barely. Getting back to being unemployed, I got to spend quality time with my daughter, who was just over a year old at the time. That was great. Plus, I did not have to wear a tie every day or any day for that matter. And it gave me a chance to update my resumé a minimum of three or four times per week. "I'm updating my resumé" always sounds good when one is out of work and people ask how you are spending your time. It sounds productive and meaningful. But, really, how long does it take to do that? A few minutes? A half hour? And what information does one have to add or change that is so time consuming as to take days? In many ways, the trick to applying for jobs is in the cover letter. Write one that is intriguing, provocative and leaves the reader wanting more and you will rarely not get an interview.

The question then becomes: what are some good ways to spend time when one is out of work other than actually looking for a job? Stalking someone, it seems to me, would be fun. It is almost like being a spy except you are not. Most people I know, of course, are not very experienced at this sort of thing. This is because they are either working or because they are home updating their resumés. If you are not experienced, then I suggest starting with an unsuspecting neighbor. They are like low hanging fruit. They live close by. In fact, if they live across the street, then you do not have to even bother leaving your own house. Just stare out your front window, only don't be obvious or creepy about it. Believe me, there are few things worse than creepy stalkers. Of course, if your neighbor does leave their house, then that means you have to leave yours. Like anything else, stalking is not without its own set of challenges. So, keep your shoes, coat and house keys close by. If you are going to do this right, then you must be ready to get up and go at a moment's notice. I can see some of you readers rolling your eyes right now. Already, you are thinking, this stalking business sounds like a lot of work. To that I say, stop your whining. Whining is for losers, crybabies and people like me who hate it when we run out of chocolate milk.

    In terms of the work itself, much of that depends upon you. For instance, when following your "stalkee", do you wish to take notes or perhaps simply memorize everything he or she does and their various places of destination? Recording what your stalkee does and where they go requires well organized charts and record keeping. This can be a lot of work, so adding paperwork to the actual stalking may be something you want to think about. On the other hand, stalkers can often set their own hours. The trick is in selecting a person who is fairly active though not unreasonably so. Unless you are a night owl, you do not want to stalk someone who often stays out until the wee hours of the morning. That is when stalking becomes real drudgery and even more stressful than is necessary. Remember: this is supposed to a hobby; something fun. So be careful who you select to follow. If you choose well, it can help make the time you spend looking for a paying job more enjoyable.

Another good way to pass time is to conduct a cross-reference analysis of all the daily soap operas on television. My hypothesis is that they are all actually the same show only with different sets of actors and different titles.

Fortunately, I survived the bump in the road that was unemployment and found myself back in higher education. As I write this, that was over thirty years ago. Even in zombie years that is a long time. This brings me back to my not having any master plan when it came to pursuing some kind of well-thought-out career. The truth is, by the time I graduated from high school, with what could only be generously described as a meager set of skills, my persona was still taking shape, still "finding itself." These skills, I should note, did not burst forth like a football team charging out onto the field to do battle. Rather, they poked their head up much like a prairie dog in the desert. In other words, my skills – and I use that word loosely – had all the kick-ass, can-do characteristics of an awkward sixth grader at his first mixer. And what were those so-called skills, you might ask? For lack of a better word, I will say "writing". I liked to write. But that is not to say I did it or do it well. My first regular writing effort occurred while working on my high school newspaper. Thankfully, the paper needed reporters, so being able to write well was not a prerequisite for being on the staff.

I was one of the paper's sports writers. Covering the games was easy because I was on a number of the teams: football, basketball and baseball (the big three). But do not be too impressed by that or think I was some kind of high-performing athlete. The fact is, I rode the bench more often than saw any actual game time. So, covering the teams was easy because I literally had a front row seat. Sure, I got bylines. While that was fun, what was not fun is that it did not get me any girls. At my level of sophistication at that, and most any other time of my life for that matter, even inexperienced girls knew to avoid me. In some inexplicable way, they sensed an evening with me would not be time well spent.

Anyway, in college I continued to write for the school newspaper. I covered the campus police, the student councils that helped run the residence halls, and even the administration. Yes, I enjoyed it, but, no, I do not remember causing the world or the college to sit up and take notice. Throughout my four years as an undergraduate, I stuck to my so-called plan of continuing to do what I was doing until I came upon what I really wanted to do. Now, here I am, over three score years old and I am still waiting for some "eureka!" moment. (By the way, did you know that term was supposedly first uttered over two thousand years ago by Archimedes when he discovered how to measure the volume of an irregular solid? Really? No offense to Archimedes, but I do not see that discovery as being really worthy of "eureka!" If Archimedes was eighty-seven years old and could still get an erection, then THAT would be a genuine "eureka" moment. But figuring out to measure an irregular solid? I don't think so. At best, that's a "Guess what I did today?" moment.)

My okay writing skills led me to pursue work after college as a newspaper reporter and eventually many years in public relations. To be fair, I did explore – or at least consider – other career paths that involved far less writing. One, in particular, was life as a professional baseball player. Unfortunately for me, I learned that to become a professional athlete in any sport one must actually be good. Real good. So good that the average person looks at that professional and thinks, "Hey, I could do that." It turns out I could not. Not even close. My claim to fame was playing one summer for a low level farm team of the Atlantic Braves in Hollywood, Florida. I went down there as a pitching prospect but quickly became known as the best thing to happen to batters since the bat. Batters loved me. Yes, it was discouraging. As my time with the team drew to a close, one very hot summer day I found myself in the outfield before a game shagging flies. I looked down at the ground and saw a scorpion walking by. Even though the scorpion did not stop and look up at me or even acknowledge my presence, I remember thinking, "Well, at least one of us knows where in the hell they're going." For a few moments, I admired the scorpion but also resented it a bit because I felt it seemed to have a better sense of direction than me. (I wonder whatever happened to that scorpion? Was it tempted to pick up a glove and shag some flies, too? Probably not. It is just as well. I was feeling down enough as it was at the time. I fear the prospect of being bested in baseball by a scorpion would have been too much to bare. That aside, even if it could catch flies better than me, to this day I take comfort in knowing that between the two of us, I had a better arm.)

My years in higher education have flown by. Since 1976, I have worked primarily in the administration of various institutions as well as teaching a number of classes in public relations, journalism, and writing. Throughout that time, I have been lucky enough to meet a wide range of men and women. Several years ago, I was introduced to a group of people as "the funniest guy on campus." My reaction to that has not changed. Disagreement.

Embarrassment. Looking for the nearest exit. Tongue-tied. And that was just within the first few seconds. All that aside, being called the top of anything is a lot of pressure to drop on someone's lap. Right away, people looked at me as if I would immediately launch into some knee-slapping monologue worthy of a headliner in Vegas or a comic being showcased on Comedy Central. Forget it. Believe me when I say if I were anywhere near that funny, then I really would be in Las Vegas right now. At best, I am like the office wise guy who stands around the water cooler cracking jokes at other people's expense (behind their backs, of course). I do not consider myself to be funny and never have. The fact I have made people laugh, even if it is about as often as a Smurf reproduces, is a minor miracle.

Looking back, do I label my journey from a so-so reporter for my high school paper to a wannabe baseball player to the present a "plan?" No. It was, and is, a life in which things unfolded. I have not yet decided whether this, in my case, has been a good thing. I suppose I will leave that to others (though I hope they keep their opinions to themselves). So, here I stand – actually sit. Writing. Or trying to implement what Hemingway described as the art of writing: "Applying the seat of the pants to the seat of the chair." I am the first to admit that I will never be able to occupy a chair like Hemingway. At the same time, for better or worse, during my years I have had literally dozens of thoughts, some reality-based and some not. This book is my attempt to share them with whoever or whatever might be interested. (Hmmm. I wonder if scorpions can read?) Is this book meant to be funny or slightly amusing? Maybe. I confess I have tried to make it so. I can only hope somebody agrees with me. In terms of the musings in this volume that gravitate between reality and pretend, I will leave it to the reader to determine which is which. Either way, just know what has been mine is now yours. After all, we are all sharing the same highway.

Protocol

Each day of our lives finds us in a string of scenes that, collectively, make up an entire day. In one scene, for instance, one walks into the bathroom, opens up the medicine cabinet, takes out ones toothbrush and toothpaste, apply ones toothpaste to the toothbrush and begins cleaning ones teeth. The next scene may involve making a cup of coffee, preparing to eat a bowl of cocoa-puffs or begin deciding what clothes to wear that day. And so it goes.

    These scenes are routine. We require little direction as the behavior that defines them leaves little room for conflict or confusion. Sure, we may have trouble deciding whether to wear the Hawaiian shirt or the more conventional white button-down one to the job interview, but the matter of whether a shirt should be worn at all is not really an issue. The point is a number of the scenes we play out in life require very little thought or intense internal debate. (It is not like being a contestant on The Price is Right, for example, where you have only moments to decide whether to go "higher" or "lower" on estimating the retail price of something while surrounded by a screaming audience and being watched by millions of viewers. That kind of pressure is not unlike trying to make love to your wife while the family dog sits in the room watching. Let's face it. That can be a bit unsettling and even intimidating. Instead of trying to please your wife, you end up trying to impress the dog. Yet the dog – and I respect this – maintains the same expression and demeanor that he displays while watching you tie your shoes. Are the two acts the same to the dog? Does the dog view your ability to make love as being no greater than your ability to tie shoes? Sadly, there seems to be no way of knowing. Dogs, and this is where they are very clever, do not tip their hand (or is it paw?). They seem unwilling to toss us a bone (pardon the expression) by coming up with a communication system where they give us feedback on how we are doing (much like the judges at an Olympic gymnastic event). Granted, I do not expect the dog to hold up cards with some kind of point value (8 points for kissing, 1.5 for foreplay, 0.5 for not taking off your black socks, etc.), but perhaps they could come up with some kind of barking system: one bark is low, two barks is okay, three barks is "hey, look at you!" and a howl is "do I have a great master or what!"

Interestingly, dogs do not seem to mind when we watch them having sex. In fact, they even seem to flaunt their ability to perform before an audience. I will even go so far as to say they seem oblivious to the watchful eyes of others. Are they that confident in their love-making abilities? Do they view themselves as being second-to-none when it comes to the art of making whoopee? We may be the master but when it comes to sex that table sure seems to be turned – and not in our favor. Maybe in some deep part of ourselves we are jealous of our dogs when it comes to lovemaking. This could be one big reason we seem so willing – dare I say even eager – to have dogs neutered.)

But I digress. There are situations during the course of a day when things are not so pro-forma when it comes to handling them or in knowing what to do. Situations arise and, with them, come questions of protocol. In science, protocol represents a predefined written procedural method of conducting experiments. Medical protocol speaks to the conducing of several meetings which result in the formulation of set treatment. In communication, it can be a set of rules and regulations that determine how data is transmitted via computer networking. All that is fairly clear. But then there are moments or times in life that are not well defined. These do not have a virtual GPS that provides one with specific instructions on what to do or where to go.

One example of this came to me several summers ago when my cousin and I were hiking down the Grand Canyon. First of all, let me say this is quite a challenge and a great deal of fun. The Grand Canyon is breathtakingly beautiful and needs to be seen to be truly appreciated. Hiking down and up it adds a much deeper appreciation to this great natural wonder. That aside, as we were hiking down I wondered what I would do if my cousin – for whatever reason – fell over the edge to his death. What is the protocol on this? What should I do? Finish the hike down? Turn around and hike back up the damn thing? Should I stop altogether? And suppose I hike down and am unable to find his body? Then what? After having tried to tell people what happened, yet not finding anyone to believe my tale because of my inability to show any evidence, then what do I do? Should I carry on as if things are normal? From a practical standpoint, does his untimely death resolve me of my commitment to complete the hike? Again, what is the protocol?

As I write this, I am thinking that perhaps where he fell over might dictate whether I carry on with the hike. For instance, if he falls over near the top, then for me to trek all the way down there seems a bit silly. Or would it? But if he fell near the bottom, then I suppose there is a chance he might still be alive, so I suppose that dictates I continue the hike. In that case, there is probably some unwritten rule that says I should pick up the pace of the hike. But if I have been hiking in the blistering sun for, say, four hours, then suddenly picking up the pace is going to be difficult. No offense to my cousin, but I am not sure I would want to quicken my hiking pace. It may not be healthy for me. At this point, it seems to me the onus is on him to take care of his own injury until I arrive. I just hope when I got there he would not be squealing like some injured piglet. Either that or I hope when I arrive he is not in the middle of being eaten by a pack of wolves. First of all, I would probably be too tired to fight them off – assuming I could in the first place – and secondly, I would not have any weapons, such as a mace, a hand grenade or a drone missile launcher, to use against them. Besides, even if I did chase the wolves away, then my cousin would probably be an absolute mess at that point. Who would want to deal with that?

A second situation regarding protocol is similar to my first example. This one, however, takes place in a restaurant. What is the protocol when you are in the middle of a meal with a companion and they have a heart attack? Let me again use my cousin. Over the years the two of us have had meals in restaurants together. Plus, as he is older than me, the odds of him being the one who falls over a ledge or has a heart attack seem to be higher than it being me. Besides, writing about scenarios involving his death is far more enjoyable than ones in which I die. (Let him write his own book.)

So, the two of us are eating and talking and occasionally using silverware when he suddenly grabs his chest, says something haunting like "Rosebud" and dies. At this point, it would not matter if he falls face first into his soup or falls out of his chair. The bottom line is I am sitting there with a half-eaten french fry in one hand and a beer in the other. Knowing me, I would probably finish the french fry before letting out with an, "Oh my God!" or "Auntie Em, Auntie Em!" or "Oh, for Chrissake's." Though similar to the first example, this one is a bit trickier as it involves payment of the meal. (And don't get me started on the tip. Given that my dinner partner just died, does that release me of any unspoken obligation I have to tip the waiter? I suspect the waiter might be wondering the same thing. "Until that guy died, I was really giving them great service. Now what?")

The big dilemma, though, is payment of the meal. If my cousin and I were each paying our own way, then am I obligated to now pick up his portion of the final bill? Suppose we had gone out the night before and I had paid for dinner then? On this particular night it was his turn to pick up the tab. But he's dead and now I'm stuck. That does not seem fair. If I mention to management that tonight actually was to be his treat so I didn't bring any money with me, then either they will think I'm lying or being an insensitive jerk for taking advantage of this unexpected tragedy. Let's face it. His untimely death would in all likelihood put me in an awkward spot.

Before continuing, I hope no one gets the impression I am a person who is self-absorbed and, consequently, thinks only of himself when tragedy befalls others. That is certainly not the case. In fairness to me, in each of the above-mentioned circumstances the death of my cousin does affect me, so of course I am going to think about me. Sure, I will think of my cousin, too, but – again, in fairness to me – with my cousin's demise, how much thinking about him do I really need to do?

The following is another situation – this one real – that involves protocol. (I use the present tense here because as of this writing it remains unresolved.) It takes place at the gym of which I am a member. I try to go there every day, though I am not sure that is apparent to anyone who sees me. Nevertheless, I am a regular and, with a few exceptions, usually go around the same time every day. Consequently, I end up seeing the same regulars almost every day. For the most part, my only interaction with any of them is a friendly nod as they – like me – are there to work out, not socialize. Socializing seems to be for the folks who actually work at the gym. They seem to be having a great time chatting with each other while the rest of us are either working up a sweat or are least trying to. Also, I should note, I have a set routine I follow and, generally, when I do go to the gym I have only a limited amount of time to spend there. Finally, I should preface this little story with the heads-up that it involves cancer. That, I realize, is never a topic of humor unless there is a definitive happy ending and even then one must tread carefully when one attempts to extract humor out of it. Generally, in terms of humor, cancer is a topic one should avoid much like child molestation, bunions, and okra.

In my time, I have had the experience of telling a joke before a large audience – and small ones, too – and have the attempt fail miserably. That moment when you tell the punch line and are waiting for a laugh that does not come is agonizing. Many years ago I was an after-dinner speaker and told a joke about a young Indian boy who longed to be with his true love, but in order to do so he had to swim across a vast lake. One day, he finally mustered enough courage to do so. Halfway across the lake he drowned. So, to this day – and here's the punch line – the lake is called "Lake Stupid". That joke is as bad today as it was when I first told it. When I did tell it, I distinctly remember the audience of several hundred people just sitting in their seats staring at me. Looking back, probably the best thing for me to have done then would have been to set fire to myself. Unfortunately, I lacked the wherewithal to do that, not to mention the nerve to no doubt violate a fire code of some sort. Anyway, it was far from one of my shining moments. I can only hope the people present have since forgotten about it. (Full disclosure: this was and is not the only time I have laid the proverbial show business egg.)

This, then, brings me to my cancer story. There is one fellow – a nice guy – about my age and with whom I do more than nod at. Not every time, but once in a while the two of us will exchange pleasantries. Recently, I learned his wife has been battling breast cancer. As one would expect, it has been a challenging time for both him and his wife. (Presently, she seems to be doing well, so that's a good thing.) So, when this man and I do chat, usually I ask about his wife. What is becoming an issue for me – a protocol issue – is the fact with each passing day this guy's answer seems to be getting longer and longer. Details piled upon details. This has put me in an awkward position. On the one hand, I do want to be polite and get an overview of how both him and his wife are. But on the other, this guy's answers are beginning to cut into my gym time. Granted, he is talking about an important thing, but at the same time I haven't got all day. I find myself starting to avoid him. But when we do talk, I listen without interruption. This is becoming harder and harder. My protocol question revolves around the best way of removing myself from this conversation. What is the best way to politely get out of his monologue without hurting his feelings or looking as if I am being uncaring?

Personally, and he may not fully appreciate it, I feel as if he is taking advantage of me here. Hearing a personal cancer story is one of those things one does not interrupt or walk away from. It is like having someone confess that the night before they caught their brother-in-law drowning several puppies in the bathtub. One cannot exactly say, "That's great, Bob, but I gotta squeeze in a few more leg lifts." Put yourself in my shoes. You are listening to a person's cancer story, yet you are on a tight schedule. And they won't stop droning on about hair loss, lack of appetite or the cost of various medicines. What is the protocol here?

In fairness to cancer, I will say this: it is a cool disease in the sense it generates sympathy. You tell someone, particularly a woman, either you have cancer or a loved one of yours does and immediately their reaction ranges from giving you a hug to wanting to have a love child with you or, at the very least, go home and make you a tuna casserole. On the other hand, there are other diseases or conditions that illicit no positive reaction. Using me as an example, a little over a year ago I came down with gout. (I now have to take what I will call an anti-gout pill every day for the rest of my life.) Gout is not an exciting or sexy disease. It does not even sound alluring. In fact, it sounds like an old man's disease. (Point of fact: gout can be quite painful and leave one hobbling around much like one of those old guys on his way to a half-price, blue plate special at the local diner. Also note that I am in no way suggesting a connection between my having gout and it being associated with old men. Me being an old guy? Even the thought of that is ridiculous.) Anyway, mentioning to another person – a woman – that you have gout triggers no response at all. "Oh, okay," is the best one gets. As a result, I have long since given up trying to score points with anyone by playing the gout card. My own sense tells me one would have better luck playing the prickly heat card.

Finally, there is one more scenario involving protocol that I have been struggling with for years. From time to time, I will be chatting with someone who is getting ready to move. They have either purchased a house or are moving into a new apartment. Naturally, upon hearing this my immediate reaction is to volunteer to help. "Just let me know, Jim, and I'll be happy to help," is usually what I will say. The person always nods, says how much they appreciate that and then thanks me. It is, by any standard, a very positive exchange. The only problem is I did not mean what I just said. Not a word. The last thing I want to do is get up early on a Saturday morning, connect with a bunch of people I do not know, lug a bunch of boxes up and down flights of stairs, make several round trip drives from the old place to the new place, and end up wasting a Saturday that I could have spent at home sitting in front of my television watching whatever happens to be on cable. Upon hearing this, one might ask me why I would even volunteer to help my friend move in the first place. The answer is obvious: because they are my friend and because I want to come across as a nice guy. The problem is I just do not want to have to prove it. Consequently, the absolute last thing I want is to have this friend actually take me up on my offer.

The protocol question revolves around what to do if they do call. What if they do ask me to help? How can I get out of it without appearing to be two-faced or, better yet, still having them think of me as a nice guy? I confess this is a tough one. There is a part of me that feels that just making the offer is a good enough demonstration of support. Granted, the offer will not actually get my friend moved, but isn't that his problem? To me, there are few things worse in the world than insincerity. But I do not see that applying to me in this case. My offering to help is a sincere gesture that I happen to be insincere about. See the difference? Is it my fault my friend cannot tell the difference? I do not think so. I am being a good friend here. There is no reason for me to feel guilty about that. Perhaps one thing I could do if he does call is to play the gout card. I bet that would finally get me the kind of response I am looking for. Okay. Problem solved. Good talk. Thank you.

A Cat Story

I love Mister Purr. I fell in love with him the moment I saw him four years ago with his brothers and sisters snuggling up to their mother. The litter of kittens was less than a day old. They were in our neighbor's garage and were just starting to get used to their new world. Fred's son, Edgar, came running over to our house saying Lilly – the mother cat – had just given birth to a new litter. We all knew she was expecting. That was no surprise 'cause that cat was always running loose. I always told my husband that if she was a human, then Lilly would be one of those no-good whores who hangs around the loading docks on a Friday night. I never liked Lilly because she was always coming over into our yard. I don't know why 'cause every time I saw her I would chase her away.

I remember asking our doctor if there was such thing as a feline whore. He said he wasn't sure, but I am. At least I am about Lilly. What kind of name is that for a cat, anyway? As soon as we could, we adopted Mister Purr right away. I say "we," but actually I was the one who adopted him. My husband is more of a dog person. He and Bucky – our dog – are always doing things together. For instance, my husband likes to take Bucky down to the dockyards 'cause he says Bucky enjoys the smell of the water. Other times, my husband likes to go to other parts of the city because he enjoys many of the night lights. He says red is his favorite color. Despite Bucky, my husband was fine with the addition of Mister Purr to our family. In fact, he even let me name the cat. That was such an easy decision because Mister Purr's whiskers are so cute and he is always purring. In fact, he's cute all over. His hair is a grayish white mixed with black patches on his legs and one on the left side of his face.

I take Mister Purr everywhere with me which is something my husband encourages. With one exception. And God bless my husband for this. He told me not to go down to those dockyards because cats don't like water. And this leads me to one of my favorite stories about Mister Purr. One summer we traveled out west to visit my favorite aunt and uncle. My husband urged me to go 'cause he knows how much I miss them. He even said I could stay as long as I liked. So, I bought myself a ticket and even arranged with the airlines to take Mister Purr with me and be in the passenger seat next to me. Of course, he had to be placed in one of those carrier-on boxes. But I didn't mind – and I don't think he did too much either – 'cause we were able to look at each other through the openings in the box. It was fine.

Our airplane was somewhere over the middle part of the country when suddenly three men with guns leaped out of their seats. (Not one of them was in first class. They were back in the passenger section like me.) They all started screaming for everyone to sit down. I thought that was odd because all of us were already seated. Actually the man in front of me had just gotten up – to go to the bathroom, I guess – but he sat right back down. And then another one of the gunmen yelled for no one to do anything funny. I thought that was odd, too, because why would any of us do anything funny, or even think of anything funny, with guns being pointed at us by strangers?

Within moments, there was a lot of screaming from most everyone around me. I'm not sure if anyone in first class screamed. It's hard to say. But I did notice that one of the gunmen had forced his way into the pilot's cabin. That's when we heard gunfire followed by more screaming. No question about it, this was serious. None of us knew what was going to happen, where we were going, or if this meant we weren't going to get any complementary drinks or peanuts.

The three gunmen all seemed young in age. At least to me. I'm guessing they were in their late twenties or perhaps early thirties. None of them were very big. In fact, they all seemed pretty thin to me and fairly short. No string beans. One was slightly bald while the other two had what I call "longish" hair though nothing like any hippies. In terms of how they treated us passengers, not one of them came even close to being as polite as our stewardesses.

The plane rocked back and forth a bit but then I heard someone say that one of the gunmen was now flying the plane. Thank goodness. I remember thinking if there is anything I definitely do not want it is to be on an airplane without a pilot. I can't remember how much time had gone by since the gunmen made themselves known, but it occurred to me I had not checked on Mister Purr. I looked down at his cage and the door was open. Mister Purr was not inside! My first reaction was absolute panic. I looked under our seats but he was not there. I poked my head up and surveyed the scene to see if I saw any sign of him. I called out his name several times until one of the gunmen came over to me with an angry look on his face. He threatened to "smash my face if I didn't shut up."

It is here where my serving for four years as secretary of our community association kicked in. I remained calm and explained that my cat was missing. It had gotten out of the carry-on bag.

"Lady, I don't give a shit about your cat. If I see it I'll shoot it," he spat back at me.

It was all I could do to not get angry. I tried to explain that the cat had done nothing to him. He was a poor animal. And just when I was going to talk about how cute and adorable Mister Purr was, the man shoved me back into my seat. I landed with a thud. I sat there and stewed awhile. I also did not like it that no one else seemed to be upset that Mister Purr was missing.

I sat there in my seat both angry and worried. Two of the gunmen kept walking up and down the aisle of the plane waving their guns and yelling at anyone and everyone. The third gunman was flying the plane. After a while, though, one gunman positioned himself in the first class section while the other stayed with the rest of us. As best I could, I kept trying to look ahead of me and behind for any signs of Mister Purr. Usually, he is always looking to sit in my lap but the fact he was not doing that this time told me even he knew things were not right. It was then that things took a sharp turn for the better, not just for me but for everyone on the plane. Except the gunmen. It all happened so fast, too.

There was a sudden screeching sound that burst throughout the plane almost as startling as a thunderclap. I saw this blur coming from one of the overhead compartments. It landed on the gunman who was stationed in the passenger section. It was Mister Purr! He leaped onto the back of the neck of the gunman.

The gunman was obviously caught off guard. He tried to spin around and yank Mister Purr off. But it did not work. Mister Purr reached around to the front of the man and proceeded to slash his throat. Mister Purr dug his front claws into the bad man's throat – deeper and deeper – until this guy with the gun fell over in a heap. Blood streamed out of his torn neck. Even though his right leg was twitching, I knew he was dead or close to it.

"Oh, Mister Purr," I exclaimed without realizing it. But Mister Purr did not have time to give me one of his loving "meows". It was clear he was on a mission to stamp out the evil on our plane. My beloved cat flipped the dead man's rifle over his shoulder and raced down the aisle toward the first class section. He had taken out the first gunman so quickly that many did not even know what had happened. My cat raced down the aisle until he came to the curtain that separated us from the first class section. At that point, Mister Purr stopped abruptly and swung the rifle into firing position. Because I was a number of rows behind him, I could not see exactly everything he did. But I do know this: he stood up on his hind legs and fired the rifle. It was not till later that I learned he had pumped several bullets into the head and chest of the second gunman, killing him instantly.

At this round of gunfire went off, it triggered more screams from the passengers, mostly the ones in first class. I could not help but think that my companion may have been riding in the passenger section, but he was a first class cat all the way.

This left only one gunman – the one flying the plane. But this did not stop Mister Purr from doing what had to be done. What happened exactly I can't say one hundred per cent for sure, since my view was blocked by other passengers and because it happened so quickly. I am only going by what was told to me by some of the first class passengers. Apparently, the door to the pilot's cockpit was already open. The gunman flying the plane had killed the pilot and co-pilot, two men I never did meet. When Mister Purr shot the second gunman, supposedly the one flying the plane got up from his seat to see what was going on. He was not carrying his rifle probably because he assumed he and his buddies were the only ones with guns. Also, I assume it is difficult to fly a large plane and carry a gun at the same time. Just as he did with the second gunman, Mister Purr pumped several bullets flush into the chest of that final baddie. The blow from the bullets knocked him back into the control panel and then he fell face first into the open doorway. Dead.

    Mister Purr had killed all three of the terrorists! I was so proud of him. But my story does not end there. With the death of bad guy number three, we were left without a pilot. All of us passengers were so happy to have the gunmen gone, but the matter of landing safely now was our big worry. But we did not worry for long. Mister Purr once again knew what to do. After he dispatched the final gunman, he did not slow down to let the passengers pet him or stroke his tail even though he enjoys those things. Mister Purr did not even wait for me to come to his side. He moved quickly to the cockpit, jumping over the dead body and leaped onto the pilot's seat.

    To this day, no one seems to know exactly how Mister Purr landed the plane. But land it he did. From what I later read in the newspapers, even the grounds control people were shocked when they saw our big 747 flying in and execute from what I understand was a near-perfect landing. As soon as the seatbelt lights went off, everyone on the plane, especially me, cheered. I told as many people as I could that Mister Purr was my cat. Soon they were congratulating me as much as Mister Purr even though I wasn't the one who slashed the throat of one gunman, shot to death the other two, and landed the plane.

As soon as I could I called home to tell my husband what had happened, but forgot it was Friday night and that's when he takes Bucky out. But we talked the next morning. By then, he had heard about it on the news. Still, I enjoyed telling him what happened. All this happened almost a year ago to this day. Every time I think about it I smile and give Mister Purr a big love squeeze. He is such a special cat and I love him so.

Questions

If there is one thing life has it is mysteries; a ton of questions that go unanswered every day. Sometimes I wonder if there is anyone other than me who even ponders them. I am not talking about big questions such as the location of Genghis Khan's burial site, how Stonehenge came to be, or who really sunk the Battleship Maine. (Another big question revolves around how Smurfs mate but I will leave that to others to ponder and address.) My questions revolve more around day-to-day stuff. Over the years, a number of these I have raised with others and from the reactions I get, people tend to treat them as they would a fly that shows up uninvited at a picnic. The fact that no one else seems to be wrestling with them does not make me feel special. Rather, it worries me. These are serious questions, dammit, that cry out for in-depth review. In no particular order, following is a partial list of what I am currently wrestling with:

* Ugly Vampires. How come there are no ugly vampires? Why is it the only vampires we see and read about are either hot babes or sexy guys? What's that all about? Does that mean those of us who do not even register on the good-looking scale because of our, uh, looks or weight are not good enough to be

turned into vampires? Does it mean we do not have to worry about being bitten by a vampire? So, may I assume it is okay for us to invite a vampire into our house or go out after dark and wander around without concern of these creatures? I guess we should feel relieved. Maybe. Yet at the same time, why is it I feel insulted instead? Don't get me wrong. I have absolutely no desire to be bitten by a vampire even though the thought of a good looking female "creature of the night" nibbling on my neck is a bit titillating. Still, no thanks. But who are these vampires to say people like me are not up to their standards in the looks department? Excuse me? At least I can see my own reflection in the mirror and make sure my tie is straight, my shirt is tucked in and hair is combed. That's gotta count for something.

*Angry Werewolves. Since we just discussed vampires, it seems only natural to slide over into werewolves. How come these creatures always seem to be so angry? They always have a chip on their shoulder and seem ready and willing to take it out on any one they come across. Why? Aren't werewolves really just big dogs? "Who's a good boy? Yes you are. Yes you are." I bet they would love having their tummies rubbed and ears scratched. And taking them for a ride in the car with the window down would no doubt send them into ecstasy. Two things: we need to give werewolves a new look-see and they need to get over being so angry.

* Playing Opossum. Have you ever driven down the road and seen a dead opossum on the side? My question is: how do you know it is dead? How do you know it is not just playing opossum? After all, without question opossums are acknowledged as being

the best in the world at this game. How do I know this? Easy. Because the game of pretending you are dead when you are really not is named after them! You see this critter on the side of the highway and do not think, "Oh. It's playing giraffe," or, "It's playing wildebeest."

I must say having an actual game named after you has got to be one of the best things ever. For instance, how great would it be to hear someone say to their young son, "Hey let's go out and play a game of Bill Watson?" You hear that knowing that society has deemed you – Bill Watson – as being so pitch-perfect at this game that you have, in essence, become the game. You and the game are one. I can only imagine this is how opossums must feel every time they hear the expression, "playing opossum". But I wonder: is this something they are born being so good at or is their expertise handed down from generation to generation? If so, how long does it take an adult opossum to teach their offspring to carry on in such an excellent manner? Furthermore, assuming opossums do this, then not only are they the best at playing dead, but they are also world champs at teaching.

* Whole Wheat. So many sandwich lovers these days, in the name of being healthy, ask for whole wheat bread. There is nothing wrong with that, but suppose someone does not want to go all the way with wheat? Does it have to be an all or nothing proposition? How come we don't have half-wheat?

* Swordfish. It is always fun watching two mighty animals go at each other. For instance, when two rams butt heads, it is hard not to watch. I bet watching swordfish duke it out would be

especially entertaining, too. I say that because instead of the traditional way of fighting, I bet they would duel. What else could they do? It would be like watching a rerun of the old Robin Hood movie where Errol Flynn and Basil Rathbone swordfight to the finish.

* Viking Funerals. The sad truth about life is that it always ends in death. The same is true with marriage, but that's another story. People die every day, sometimes at their home, sometimes in the hospital and sometimes as an opening act in Vegas. Death is never fun. Neither are funerals. In fact, one of the great ironies of life is the fact the word "fun" is found in funeral. I suppose it is too late to change that but maybe if our planet is ever taken over by an alien race, then maybe that could be one of their do-overs. Coinciding with our ever rising death toll is the business of disposing of bodies. For me, my intention is to donate my body to science. Overall, I am okay with that though there is part of me that worries that a class full of smartass college students will take one look at my naked remains and start making jokes at my expense. Whether that is right or wrong, I am not totally sure. But I do believe strongly it would not be fair. Being dead, I won't be able to cover up nor defend myself. It will be like reliving the gang showers I took after football practice in high school. Talk about hell. It is too bad taking a shower with other teenagers is not an Olympic sport because I am sure I broke several land-speed records getting in and out during that time.

Once again, I digress. There are those who choose to be disposed of in the traditional way by being buried. Nothing wrong with that though I still do not get the point of shelling out for an expensive casket. Others choose to be cremated. That's fine, too. It is done in another room away from onlookers. The body is brought out in an urn and that, as the man once said, is that. Of course, what people do with the ashes is a big challenge all by itself. I'm not sure what I would want done with my ashes. Keep them in the urn or spread them around somewhere? That's a tough one.

Nowadays, there seems to be one style of funeral that no one ever goes for any more. That's right. The Viking Funeral. I can't say I totally understand why. When one thinks of how elaborate some weddings are these days, then it is surprising no one goes this route when it comes to sending a loved one off to the hereafter. Let's be honest, there is a majestic quality to a Viking funeral that is hard to top. The body is laid out on a fancy raft surrounded with beautiful floral arrangements. They are then pushed out into the open sea. As the mourners watch, several designated archers proceed to shoot flaming arrows into the raft, perhaps even into the body. Within seconds the body and raft are exploding with flames. Even the saddest of the mourners can't help but "oohh" and "aaahhh" over such a sight. Plus, if you add music to all this – something by Mozart or one of the Bachs – then you in all likelihood have turned a somber occasion into one that family and friends will talk about for a long time.

The trick, of course, is to hire competent archers. The last thing you want is to have someone who has trouble hitting the target. Granted, the target is moving but not all that fast. If the raft with the deceased floats too far away from shore, then someone – perhaps a distant uncle or two – can be on hand in a small motor boat to retrieve the floating item and bring it back to shore. Yes, having to re-launch the raft and body would be awkward, but it beats having an unattended corpse on a raft left to the whims of the sea and its currents. Besides, how freaked out would it be for an unsuspecting family on a snorkeling adventure to come across such a raft with its content?

One final word on this: I don't think we should no longer have Viking funerals because there aren't any Vikings left. Elvis has been dead for many years now, but people still dress like him and try to perform like him. I am sure they do that in tribute to his achievement in the entertainment world. Viking funerals can be done to honor not just the deceased but Vikings as well. It's a win-win. But be sure and hire archers who know what they're doing.

* The Kongs. There have been plenty of movies featuring King Kong. But what about his brother, Hong? He's gotta be worthy of an introduction to the world, and then a sequel just to capitalize on all the money the first one makes. Besides, it would be interesting to see if Hong has a weakness for blondes like his brother.

* "Seize her!" I wonder if the following moment of confusion ever happened in the days when Julius Caesar was emperor of Rome:

A female prisoner is brought before the great Caesar. He gazes down upon her from his royal chair and says, "So, we finally have you."

Suddenly, without warning, she leaps up, shoves several of her guards aside and makes a bee-line for the nearest exist. One of the enterprising young guards calls out, "Seize her!"

"What?" says Caesar.

"Ah, no your royal greatness. I wasn't talking to you."

"Then why you impudent snot did you call my name?" Caesar bellows.

The guards suddenly freeze where they are. Rarely have they heard the Great Caesar raise his voice in such a manner and never have they heard any one address him in such a way.

"But, sire, I did not call your name," the guard stammers. He looks around and sees the girl getting closer to the exit. "Seize her!" he cries out again.

"What?" screams Caesar.

"No, your Excellency. Her. Not you."

"Do not talk to me with such a tone! Are you saying I do not know my own name? Are you saying I am daft?" Casear says rising from his throne.

"No... No... Of course not. It's she. I mean it's you..." the guard responds.

"Take this fool to the tower right now. We will deal with him promptly," commands Caesar.

Several of the other guards quickly bop the man over the head and body with clubs and then drag him out of the room...

"Wait. Wait a minute... I can explain... There's been a misunderstanding," the guard cries out as he is dragged from the royal throne room.

"This is outrageous," one of Caesar's top advisors whispers to the emperor.

Caesar shakes his head in frustration. "I want us to make an example of him to all the others," he says. "How dare he or any one question my mental capacity."

"Yes sir," the advisor responds.

"How did this guy even get hired?" Caesar asks.

The adviser clears his throat. "Uh, your highness, I believe he was recommended by your brother-in-law."

"Oh for God's sake. No wonder," Casear throws up his arms. "Now where were we? Oh, right. Bring in the female prisoner!"

The remaining guards scan the room. The girl is long gone.

* New Breeds. What's the deal with people who create new breeds of animals? Are they bored? Are the existing breeds no longer enough for them? A case in point is the labradoodle. What the hell is that, you may ask? At least that is what I asked when first told of its existence. To me, it sounds like something one of the characters from a Harry Potter book says when attempting to cast a spell on a bad witch. Do we really want breeds that make any of us scratch our heads and say "huh?" Aren't there enough confusing things in the world already? Don't most of us spend at least part of our days slightly confused anyway? (Or is it just me?) Actually, the labradoodle is a crossbred dog created by crossing a labrador retriever with a miniature poodle. Apparently, this mixture was concocted to serve as an allergen-free guide dog. In other words, it was created to provide a pet for people with allergies to fur and dander. Who knew? Does that mean this dog won't guide people who are not allergic to fur and dander? Shouldn't we be the ones who turn dogs down instead of the other way around? All that aside, apparently a lot of people are quite comfortable with the labradoodle. If you don't believe me, then check out the Australian Labradoodle Association and even the Australian Labradoodle Club of America. (I wonder what they talk about at their meetings?) Plus, there are those who are attempting to create a whole new breed of dog by breeding these dogs with each other over successive generations. I hope this is

all they have in mind. I hope that old bug-a-boo world domination is not part of their long-range plan.

The labradoodle is but one example of a different kind of dog being bred to create a new breed. Examples of these other kind of hybrid or designer dogs include mixtures of a schnauzer and poodle (known as a Schnoodle), a pug and a beagle (known as a Puggle), and a German shepherd and a husky (known as a German Chusky). This seems to be getting out of hand. I say that because breeders have even put together a chihuahua and dachshund and are calling it a Chiweenie. That cannot be right. What self-respecting person would even admit to owning a Chiweenie?

If left to me, I would have cross-bred Lassie with Rin Tin Tin and called it Super Dog. Not only would I give this new critter a fancy collar to wear but I would have it wear a bright – perhaps red – cape. Why not? Weren't Lassie and Rin Tin Tin our two greatest canines? After all, they both made movies, had their own television shows, and had multiple books of their various adventures written about them.

I have been blessed with having a couple of great dogs in my life: first Checkers and then Dusty. As both were mutts, they, too, were the result of cross breeding. (Do not worry, reader, I am not going to bore you with tales of either dog. The only things I will say about Checkers and Dusty are "National Spelling Bee" and the "Maryland State Fair Best Pie Baking Contest" and leave it at that.)

Speaking of pets, I think a great pet name would be "Peeve". Get it. When you have company you could say, "Here's my pet, Peeve." I do not think that would ever get old.

* "People Person." Why do some people insist upon describing themselves as a "people person?" Aren't we all people persons? After all, we are people. Besides, what is the alternative: chipmunk person? lampshade person? Where does it end? Granted, some may not enjoy the company of other humans all that much, but it does not make them any less of a people person. Sometimes students I teach describe themselves that way and I always – in a gentle and hopefully kind way – strongly urge them to stop doing that. While we may not all be able to get along, we are what we are: two-legged creatures with the ability to make music and change our minds. Additionally, interacting with our own kind brings out the best in us (and the worst). So, let that be our focus while extending kindness to the creatures of the world that do not share our biological classification. (I promise to make that my only editorial comment in this book.)

* Turtle Love. Suppose you are walking along and notice a turtle in the middle of having intercourse with a rock? After taking a few moments to watch, point and giggle, and then take a picture of it on your i-phone, what do you do? Giving the turtle the benefit of the doubt that it is not a pervert sexually attracted to rocks, what do you do? Do you gently remove the turtle from the rock or do you let it finish? The quick answer here may be to simply let it finish. After all, it is just a turtle we are talking about and what is the harm anyway? On the other hand, as experts generally agree that turtles are monogamous creatures, then this suggests the turtle you have sighted is in the process of mating with the great love of its life. How sad. It seems to me the dilemma is as follows: should you let the turtle stay with the rock and thus go the rest of its long life with what will at best become an unsatisfying relationship? Or do you stop the turtle in the middle of its passion, thus risking giving it some kind of sexual trauma and – perhaps even worse – ruining it for future relationships the turtle might have because it has been taken away from what it feels is the true love of its life? Part of the answer depends upon the sensitivity of the turtle. If it is removed from the rock, will it be forever heartbroken for having lost the "female" of its dreams? Or will the turtle chalk up what happened to experience, get back in the dating game, and eventually give its heart to another? The fact that turtles are apparently so faithful makes this a tough call for the person who spots the turtle and the rock.

In this case, perhaps it is best to let the turtle make its own choice and then deal with it as best it can. I do not see this so much as practicing "tough love" as I do of having faith the turtle knows its heart. After all, who are of any of us to question the love between others? Sure, they may have problems. For instance, at some point the turtle is going to be frustrated at the fact the rock is not giving him any baby turtles or that the rock never seems to want to go anywhere. Nevertheless, if it is meant to be, then the turtle and the rock will make their relationship work.

* Goldfish and Parrots. Speaking of pets, there are several I don't get. This little segment, then, is not so much a question as it is a puzzlement. Specifically, I speak of the goldfish and parrot. To be fair, the goldfish does deserve a big shout-out. Is there any living creature that comes as close to being maintenance-free as the goldfish? Off-hand, I can't think of any. Other than feeding them once a day and changing their water whenever you feel like

it, that's about it. Plus – and I do not mean this as a criticism even though it is true – goldfish do not exactly bring out the affectionate side of us. They swim around in circles with a seeming indifference to the size of their bowl or whether we are in the room with them. Even cats acknowledge our existence from time to time. But not goldfish. Also, it does not help that their life expectancy seems to be about an hour and a half. (Okay. I may be exaggerating here but not by much.) I look at goldfish and think: "Where's the love?" I feel like I could be lying on the kitchen floor choking on a celery stick and they would not care. (Unlike a dog that would be absolutely frantic. Another thing about dogs is they practically have an orgasm when we walk into the house after being gone all day.) Earlier in the day, the dog could have been awarded the Nobel Prize for Physics but that would not matter the moment the pet hears the owner's voice.

"Hey, boy," the owner says. "That is so awesome about the Nobel Prize."

But the dog shakes his head. "Forget that. I want to hear about your day," he barks.

Who wouldn't love that?

This brings me to parrots. I find these birds to be somewhat disconcerting. Did you know their life expectancy is approximately eighty years! If there is any creature that puts the goldfish to shame in that category it is the parrot. That aside, I would find it unsettling to buy a pet that in all probability is going to outlive me. Granted, if one day, for fun, I am trying to see how close I can come to an airplane propeller without getting cut and miscalculate, then obviously I will meet my maker long before my pet. But I am assuming here that my calculations are correct and I live as long as I am supposed to (whatever that is). So, when I am back on the kitchen floor choking on that same celery stick and making eye contact with my pet the parrot, I do not doubt for a minute that bird is thinking something to the effect, "Don't worry about me, I'm sure your grand kids will turn out to be outstanding adults." (A few feet away, of course, the damn goldfish is totally oblivious to the drama unfolding before him.)

Under normal circumstances, which does not include sickness or getting run over by a car, dogs and cats live approximately fourteen to sixteen years. That is a good chunk of time to establish a meaningful bond with such a pet. Additionally, owners can even pick out their pet and watch it evolve into a great companion. But when it comes to the parrot, forget it. For a youngster to develop great childhood memories of that kind of pet, then their parents need to run to the pet store practically moments after conceiving the child to ensure the child will have a chance of "growing up" with the parrot. The parrot is like "old man river" when it comes to life. I am not sure I like that.

* Cats and Seeing-Eye Dogs. Do you think whenever a cat sees a seeing-eye dog on duty it knows the dog is working so it is not allowed to behave in a way a dog normally does? Given that, do you think the cat is tempted to start doing zany things just to taunt the dog, such as walk slowly back and forth in front of the dog, start doing the Charleston or perhaps doing a series of forward rolls? Even if the cat does not do any of those things, I bet it is at least thinking about it.

* In-laws. Do not worry. I am not going to string together a series of tired in-law jokes. They have been done over a million times, so there is no need to put any of us through that again.

Not here anyway. However, if I ever get my own stand-up act, then be warned you will be in for an evening of well-traveled in-law jokes and one-liners. But, as a son-in-law, something I have always struggled with is what to call them. Do you call them Mom or Dad or by their names? And is it their first names ("Come sit by me, Ken and Stephanie") or last names? ("Good talking to you, Mr. and Mrs. Blevins.") For me, in my life I have had several sets of in-laws. At no time did I call them Mom and Dad. That was never a tough call. I already had parents, so I was not going to give my wife's parents the same label as those two older adults who conceived and, for better or worse, raised me. (I am sure there were times when my Mom and Dad would have loved to have given those labels away to any takers.)

The challenge is in deciding whether to call them by their first or last names. This was always my challenge. It seemed too formal to call them by their last names, yet too informal to go the first name route. After all, it is not as if we were pals. We just have their daughter in common. Typical of me, I took the path of least resistance and never really called my in-laws anything. Backed into a corner, I would use their first names but it is something I never got used to or did very often. So, to those of you who are about to marry and are seeking advice about this whole what-to-call-my-in-laws issue, I cannot help you. It continues to be one of my life's struggles.

* Unlikeable People. Have you ever befriended someone who either does not have any friends or who is not liked by others? I have and I must say it is not fun. Sure, it may sound noble but I am not sure it is all it is cracked up to be. Being someone's only friend brings with it a great deal of pressure.

Being another person's only source of entertainment is a big burden to carry around. It is like being on-call 24/7. That's for doctors and firemen. But friends? I am not so sure. If this unlikeable/friendless person had other friends, then you could be assured of having at least a few evenings per week off-duty.

And then there is the matter of why they do not have any friends. Maybe there is a reason why no one likes them. Maybe they are annoying, not too bright, or socially inept. Maybe they eat mash potatoes with their hands. Maybe they talk during a movie. Maybe they can't hold their liquor and always end up barfing in the backseat of someone else's car. (By the way, isn't "barf" a funny word?) And if nobody likes them, then what does that say about you? If you are the only one who can stand being with them, then how likeable can you be? It seems like this might be a good time to assess your own relationships, not to mention your own habits and behavior. It is not unlike a candidate running for office. If everyone votes against them but you, then maybe – just maybe – it is you who might be a smidgen off-base.

In college, in the hope of earning three easy credits, I once took a music class that focused on choral singing. I always thought I had a decent voice, so I figured singing with a bunch of other people for an hour a couple of times a week would not be so bad. However, as the weeks passed I could not help but notice that the instructor kept shifting my position in the group. I finally learned that he kept moving me around to try and find a spot where my, uh, voice would be the least disrupting to the other singers. Finally, by mid-semester there were no other spots to move me, so I was given the task of handing out the song books to the students at the beginning of each class and then collecting them when it ended. The good news here is that the class turned out a very easy three credits, but the flip side of that was I learned my voice was far from decent. The lesson here was that there are different ways to look at a person and positions they are in and not all of them are necessarily positive.

* Naming of Animals. How did animals get their names? I am not talking about whose idea it was to name the family poodle Fifi or the pet goldfish Goldy. Rather, I am referring to the person whose idea it was to label the creature we now identify as a horse as a horse, the creature we know to be a snake as a snake, and so on. Religious-type tend to credit Adam as the one who identified all animals. Assuming that is true, then Adam really put in a couple of long days to do all that. And how did he remember what label he gave what creature? Was he writing it all down as he walked around the forest or did he have someone else taking notes on everything he said?

"Hmmm. I will call that a penguin. That's a gazelle. And that thing over there I will call, oh let me see, I'm thinking spider. And, whoa, I gotta go with elephant for that thing with the long – whatever it is – coming out of its face."

Naming all the animals had to be as exhausting as building the pyramids. Given this possibility, we can better understand how the fly got its name. My guess is it had to be near the end of a long day of animal-naming when this little creature with wings first appeared. Between yawns, Adam probably watched it for a few seconds and said, "Fly." With that, he probably flopped down on the ground and fell fast asleep counting those wooly things making that strange "baaaaahhhhh" sound.

But suppose it was not Adam who did all that? If it was not him, though, then the list of suspects is wide open. Was it a committee? And who appointed its members? Did they ever argue over a name?

If so, how were things settled?

"Gentlemen, come on. We've got to move on. What say we go with Al's choice of chimpanzee for this hairy thing and the next animal that wanders by we'll call 'buffalo'. Is that okay, Frank? By the way, Frank, how in the world did you come up with 'buffalo'? What does that even mean?"

And once all the animals were named, how difficult was it for people to get all the names right?

"Hey look, Kyle. There goes a bat."

"Ah, no Tom. I believe that was a dog."

"Are you sure? I could swear it's a bat.

"That's funny 'cause my cousin made the same mistake yesterday. Trust me. It's a dog. My neighbor, Rudy, has a friend who's brother-in-law is on the animal naming committee. He assures me that thing is a dog."

"Oh. So, what's a bat or am I just making that name up?"

"No. Bats are those sticks you hit baseballs with."

"Wait a minute. What's a baseball? What kind of animal is that?"

And so it goes. The good news is all our animal names are straight and universally accepted. In fact, that a skunk is called a skunk by Americans and Britons regardless of their political, religious or ethnic persuasion is testament to the fact that there remain things on which all people everywhere can and do agree.

* Blind Dates: In my time I have been on a few blind dates. By that I mean neither the girl nor I knew each other beforehand or even knew what the other looked like. Fortunately, at least

from my perspective, they did not turn out too badly though I have trouble remembering if there were follow up dates with any of them. Still, none of these unknowns were gargoyles in the looks department or had deadbeat personalities. (I have no doubt that if any of those ladies look back on their blind date experiences, they may think, "Mine weren't so bad except for this one guy...") My only defense at this point is that I was and will always remain a work in-progress. And I have never served time in prison, so that has got to count for something.

Looking back, going out with a stranger really does seem like a risk on both our parts. All we were going on when we agreed to go out was the word of our mutual friends and their claims we were both nice and "cute". In retrospect, that seems so thin. I wonder: did our friends really believe the two of us would make a great couple, destined for lasting love, companionship, and purchasing adjoining cemetery plots? Or were they attempting to manufacture another couple they could socialize with?

I have never been on a literal blind date in which the person I shared the evening with was without sight or literally blind. Such a circumstance raises a number of questions with the exception of one: Who's going to drive? It seems like that is something that does not even need to be discussed. But if they do offer to pick you up, what are you going to say: "I live at 2000 Summit Avenue, so pull up out front and honk"? And what happens if the blind date is late? Do you accept their excuse when they claim they missed a couple of turns or got behind some slow poke? Or suppose when they pull up onto your street and park out front, they are actually parked at 2004 Summit Avenue? Do you congratulate them for getting close, do you not say anything, or do you say respectfully but firmly: "Next time I would appreciate your parking in front of my house. There was plenty of room." But, driving aside, when one goes out with a blind person how dressed up do you really have to be? And suppose they have a seeing eye dog? Does the dog sit in the back seat? Are you allowed to pet it?

Otherwise, there is no reason to think a literal blind date won't be any nicer or any more of a disaster than any other date. As a teacher, I have had blind students in my classes and found them to be as engaging as any other student. At the same time, a few have been, shall we say, less engaged than others as well. The lesson here is except for the vision-thing, persons with poor vision or without vision have a great deal more in common with the rest of us than not.

When it comes to dating, I fear my track record has been less than stellar. Much to my regret, one evening in particular continues to stand out in my mind. (While it does not involve a blind person, a big part of it revolves around an inability on my part to see things as well as I should have.) It happened during my undergraduate years over forty years ago. I was a senior and for the first time had my own car with me. There was a girl in one of my classes I took a shine to even though I did not know her very well. She lived off campus with her parents, so we made arrangements for me to go by and pick her up at her house. So far so good.

As I pulled into her long driveway, I remember being impressed with the property. The driveway went over a small, narrow bridge that had been built over a gully approximately ten feet deep. Within moments I was at the front door. The girl's father greeted me and invited me inside. My date was upstairs getting ready so I had the pleasure of chatting with her folks. It was going pleasantly enough when the girl's father asked if I wanted a drink. At this point, he was already pouring himself a glass of scotch. Trying not to appear as if I was some rube, I calmly said I would have what he was having. He seemed a bit surprised.

"When did you learn to drink scotch?" he asked.

"Oh, for a while now," I smiled all the while thinking "never." At this point in my young life, my most decadent drink was beer.

He poured me a glass which I proceeded to empty pretty quickly. I was nearly finished with my third glass when my date – oh yeah, my date – finally came downstairs.

"Sorry," she said. "I was on the phone."

At this point, the world around me was looking a tad fuzzy. I took her arm more to keep from walking into a wall than to be polite. Everyone was all smiles as my date and I got into the car. "Everything is fine," I thought. "I've got it all under control"

With that sense of bravado, I gave the parents a final wave, smiled at my pretty date, put the care in reverse, and stepped on the gas. Without slowing down at all, I proceeded to back the car toward that little bridge. Unfortunately, I missed it and, instead, drove right down into the gully. I'm not sure which one of us yelped the loudest: my date or me. My poor car – a used Chevrolet Impala – was parked at about a forty-five degree angle and we were inside looking up at the darkening sky. At this point, I still had the presence-of-mind to both ask my date if she was all right (she was) and to be extremely embarrassed. To bring this painful memory to a close, the father helped us both out of the car and called a tow truck. I do not recall having to wait all that long before it arrived and pulled my Chevy out of the ravine with little difficulty. What I do recall is a great deal of silence as we waited for the tow truck to arrive. This proved to be my first and last date with that young lady. Even now, I sometimes think if we had just been able to make it over that damn bridge, then we would have had a good time and gone on to become one of the twosomes in history. Or maybe not. In retrospect, she would have been better off with a guy who was blind by nature rather than three glasses of straight scotch.

* 3D Glasses – I am guessing I am like a lot of other movie goers in that I enjoy watching 3D movies. More to the point, I love wearing those 3D glasses that enable you to "experience" the movie more fully. It is great when one of the characters seems to point at the audience, for instance, and you actually move your head back so as to not get poked in the eye. Given just how awesome those 3D glasses are, wouldn't it make real life so much better and realistic if we all wore 3D glasses all the time? Just imagine: experiencing life in all its dimensions just as we are meant to.

* Bad Backs: How many times have we seen someone we know bent over and in obvious discomfort. "What happened?" we ask with concern. "It's my back," they grimace. "It went out last night."

Am I the only one who wonders where backs go when they go out? Is there a back night-life that we don't know about? Are there nightclubs just for backs or are they open to all body parts? How do backs get out of the house anyway? If this is what is happening, then perhaps we ought to give them a curfew. After all, backs have a job to do, too. I suppose, though, that sort of thing is between a person and their back.

I guess the next time we see a friend or co-worker hobbling around because their back "went out," maybe their problem is not the discomfort so much as it is the fact their back went out and has not yet returned.

And, speaking of body parts, the other day I heard someone say they have a "bad shoulder." I wondered what made it bad. Was it making fun of the elbows or legs? And why was one shoulder bad and the other "good"? When you have two shoulders, aren't they like having twins? Don't you raise them the same way? Teach them the same values? Tell them it is good to share? If all that is true, then why would one be bad and the other good?

* Doggie Paddle. If it seems as if a number of my questions revolve around animals, trust me when I say that is a total coincidence, much like in college my showing up at the same spot at the same time each day for weeks on the chance I would run into that good-looking girl again. My question here revolves around organized athletics. Why isn't the doggie paddle recognized as a legitimate swimming stroke? It is certainly one of the most popular methods of going from one side of the pool to the other. You sure see people of all ages and sexes using it a lot more than you do the butterfly or breast stroke. Throw a first-time swimmer into the deep end and see what their stroke of choice is. That's right: the doggie paddle. I rest my case.

* Top Billing. There have been so many great pairs or duos throughout history. In fact, they have become so connected by the public that to mention one without the other does not feel right. For instance, is it even possible to think of Lord without

Taylor, Abbott without Costello, Laurel without Hardy, Neiman without Marcus, Sacco without Venzetti or Heckle without Jeckle? I think not. But one thing I have always wondered is how it was decided which one got top billing. Did Sears and Roebuck toss a coin or have a prolonged debate over it? Did Tom and Jerry have some kind of drinking contest to determine the order of their names? And what about Mason and Dixon? Was "Dixon-Mason line" even considered? And what about Laverne and Shirley? I suppose there are some questions in life that will never be answered and in the case of many of these and other teams, the one revolving around top billing will be one of them. Too bad.

Dark Side/Bright Days

Narrator
Can we all just admit we have a dark side? Because of that common denominator, I do not think this is anything any of us needs to be ashamed of. We think inappropriate thoughts. They give us enjoyment and make us smile. Yet if confronted with them, we would either deny we ever had them or swear on a stack of Frank Sinatra CDs that we would never ever condone them or act on them. Yet we have them and, boy, do they help us get through the day at times.

All this serves as a lead-in to my confession that I have a dark side. No, I am not confessing to secretly being some kind of evil mastermind that devises schemes to take over the world. (There are several primary reasons for this: (1) I lack the brain power and (2) I am too lazy. Oh, I guess a third reason is I am not evil. Of course, this is exactly what a person who is evil would say.) My darkness falls on the side of thinking things rather than acting on them, so in a way that is a good thing. Isn't it?

Two related examples speak to this. They both pertain to tragic incidents that happened at different times over the past few years. One has to do with a woman being mauled to death by a bear at a camp site she and her husband had set up one summer.

The other pertains to a guy and his date who went bungee jumping. The woman went over the side only to have her rope come undone causing her to fall to her death. No question about it, both incidents are horrifying and very tragic. We can only hope that neither ever happens again to anyone. Plus, our hearts go out to the families who had to endure each one.

Having said that, however, each one makes for a great story to tell at a party. All of us, of course, have been to parties. Some more than others. It is not uncommon to be standing among other folks you do not know all that well and find yourself trying to come up with something to say or talk about. You may even want those others to like you, so that makes your internal struggle to be engaging and fun all the more intense. With that in mind, how great is it for the guy whose wife was eaten by a bear before his eyes the previous summer?

Story #1

"Hi, I'm Ellen."

Ellen is an attractive, brown-haired divorcee in her mid-forties. She is slim, well groomed and has an easy smile.

"Hey there. I'm Lou. It's nice meeting you. How do you know Carl and Margaret?"

"We work in the same office. Have for several years now."

"Oh. That's great."

Lou is the protagonist of this little tale. He, too, is in his forties. He's in fairly good shape, has most of his hair, and has the persona of an unassuming, approachable guy. He is also a bit of an introvert. Only the party's hosts know what happened to his wife only months before.

Lou and Ellen exchange polite smiles. Lou looks down at his feet while Ellen scans the room trying to find someone else to talk with. They give each other another glance and exchange two more polite smiles.

"Boy, can you believe this weather?" Lou finally says.

"I know," says Ellen. "I just wish it would make up its mind. One day it's cold and the next day you feel like wearing shorts."

Lou nods and gives a little smile. Ellen nods, too. Silence follows. It is followed by more silence.

Suddenly, Carl appears before them. "Hey you two," he booms. "I see you're getting to know each other. That's great. Margaret and I wanted you two to meet. Ellen, has Lou swept you off your feet yet?"

"Well, Lou and I were just commenting on this crazy weather," she says.

"Who cares about that. Lou, tell Ellen what happened to you this summer. Ellen, it's an incredible story."

"Oh, I don't know, Carl," says Lou. "I don't want to bore anyone."

"Are you kidding? Ellen, you gotta hear this. In fact, everybody should hear this," Carl says as he waves his arms to get the attention of others. "Listen up everyone. Lou here has something to tell us."

The partiers stop talking and focus their attention on Lou. Lou shifts his position. He is not used to being the center of attention under any circumstance.

"Well, Carl is exaggerating. I don't want to bore anyone," he finally says.

"Oh come on, Lou. It'll be great," Carl says.

Lou takes a deep breath. "Okay," he begins. "Some of you may be wondering why I'm not here with the missus. This past summer Charlene and I went on our usual camping trip. It's great fun and something we've been doing for years. It was the first night of our trip and we had parked the camper and were getting unpacked. I went back to the camper to get some kitchen stuff while Charlene was near the tent finishing getting that set up. I was just about to go inside the camper when I heard this noise – it was a kind of huffing sound. I turned around and saw this bear. A black bear. Not too big, but big enough to do some real damage.

Lou chuckles. "I was going to say if you don't believe me, then ask Charlene, but you can't."

"That bear was big enough for Charlene," Carl chimes in. Several people laughed, including Lou.

"Yeah," says Lou. "Anyway, when I turned around I saw the bear standing just a few feet away from Charlene. He must have just popped out of the bushes. He was standing looking straight at her. She had this frozen look on her face as if she was screaming. Except no sound was coming out of her mouth. It was the funniest expression."

Lou looks around and everyone seemed to be gravitating toward him. They all had smiles on their faces. Even Ellen.

"So the bear reaches out and pulls her into him. She lets out with some kind of muffled noise and even tried to struggle a bit. But the bear was so strong so the kicking and flailing she was doing did not seem to matter all that much to the bear. At this point the bear started to chow down on her. It was amazing to watch," Lou continues. "I don't know how long it took. After a while, I went back into the camper and decided I might as well turn around and go home. I figured the bear was probably stuffed, so I wouldn't have trouble. Still, I then figured heading home might be the right thing to do. By the time I stepped out of the camper the bear was gone. And so, too, was Charlene. That was about it, really. I packed up and went home. But, boy, was that a sight."

The party goers applaud. Some even come over and pat Lou on the back. "That was great, Lou," beams Carl. "Did I tell you all he had a great story or what!"

The people drift back to their previous conversations as Lou stands by himself for a few moments. He is pleased to have been the center of attention in such a positive way. He hears a soft clearing of a throat and looks up. It is Ellen.

"That was great," she smiles.

"Thanks, Ellen," he smiles back.

"I really think we ought to get to know each other better," she says taking his arm.

Narrator

For one evening, the gruesome death of Lou's wife transformed this shy man into the life of a party and possibly introduced him to an evening of raw, uninhibited sex with a carefree woman who he had met only hours before. In the days that followed, Lou carried with him a lasting gratitude toward all bears everywhere.

Story #2

This story involves a young man who is fun-loving outside of the office but hard working and determined at the office. He has been working in the accounting office of his company for over four years and has been trying without success to get a promotion since year number two. He is frustrated at what he views as his inability to get a break.

Kevin puts his book case on the desk of his cubicle. He sits down and hits the on-switch to his computer. He sits back in his chair and lets out with a sigh. Another day at the rock pile, he thinks. Maybe today will somehow and in some way be different. As he stands back up he chuckles to himself. "How many times have I thought that?" he thinks.

Kevin picks up his coffee mug and heads over to the office kitchenette. As usual, he finds his office mates: Don, Mitch and Debbie. They, too, are fixing their morning cups of coffee and getting ready to get into the day.

"Morning everyone," Kevin says.

They nod back.

"Did everyone have a good weekend?" Kevin asks.

Finally, Don speaks up. "Yeah, it was fine. As usual we had to do our non-stop running taking the kids to soccer practice and then ballet. It was fine but it seems that's all Suzie and I ever do."

"Soccer and ballet don't sound all that bad to me," Debbie chimes in. "I had to take my collie to the vet for some kind of emergency procedure. It turns out it's something he ate at the dog park. God knows what. He seems to be better now but the visit cost me a fortune."

"I know. I know," Mitch adds. "I had that pug for years and spent a ton on medical bills before we finally had to put him down. That money isn't a write-off either. Straight out of pocket."

"You're telling me," Debbie moans.

The four co-workers are about to return to their cubicles when Don says, "Hey Kevin, how did your date with that hot blond go this weekend? I know you were nervous, it being a fix-up from your sister."

"Oh my God. I nearly forgot. The whole thing is unbelievable," says Kevin in a slightly raised voice.

Don, Mitch and Debbie stop in their tracks and turn facing Kevin. "Out with it, man. Tell us what happened," says Don.

Kevin clears his throat. "Her name was Jacqueline. She was really a babe just like my sister said. You know my sister. She always exaggerates but this time she was right on the money. She said Jacqueline was kind of a thrill seeker, someone who likes a good time – just like me – so she thought the two of us would hit it off. And she was right. Jacqueline was great. It was almost as if we had known each other for years. We talked and laughed at the same jokes and really felt comfortable with each other. At least that's how I felt. Well, we had already agreed to go bungee jumping because it was supposed to be a beautiful weekend and this is something apparently she had been wanting to do for years."

"Bungee jumping. You're kidding," Debbie says.

"I know. That would definitely not be my choice for a first date. I'm more of a movie and dinner kind of guy, at least on the first go-around," Kevin responds. "But I have bungee jumped a couple of times before and figured this would be all right. Even if we didn't hit it off it would at least give us something to talk about. So, we go out to the LeBlanc Bridge which is the closest spot where people around here do this sort of thing. When we got there some other couples were already there and, of course, there was this guy – a kind of guide – to supervise everything. Jacqueline was very excited and didn't seem nervous at all. I thought that was pretty impressive. We watched a couple of others go over the side and it went great. Every time it happened

Jacqueline would applaud and give out with some whoops. She was great."

"So what happened," Mitch says. "Don't stop."

"Okay," Kevin says as he takes a sip of his coffee. "Hmm. This is good stuff. Anyway, it gets to be our turn. Usually couples jump together but Jacqueline insisted she wanted to go first. She said she wanted to be able to watch me and she wouldn't be able to do that if we went at the same time. I thought that was kind of sweet."

"Yeah," Debbie sighs.

"So, we both got tied up to our ropes. Jacqueline tied her own rope. I remember watching her and thinking she seemed to be in a bit of hurry. Plus, she was joking around with everyone else and I wasn't sure if she was paying close enough attention. But then I figured that was just the accountant in me talking. Plus, she seemed so relaxed. So confident. I figured everything was fine. Well, she stands on the ledge – the jump-off point – and gives me this big big smile. Then, she yells 'Geronimo' and over she goes."

"God, why does everyone yell that?" Mitch says. "Talk about a cliché."

"Oh, I know," Debbie laughs. "And I was just starting to like her."

Kevin takes another sip of coffee. "Anyway, over the side she goes. We all looked over the edge to watch her descent. I'm not sure what happened but there was snap – it was her rope – and down down down she went. I'm not even sure if Jacqueline knew what happened. It happened so fast. Somebody who was watching – I don't know who – let out a scream. We all watched Jacqueline fall over a thousand feet to the bottom. Splat! I'm not sure what was worse: watching her hit the bottom or hearing the sound of her hitting the ground like that. I tell you it was unbelievable. It was awful. What a way to go. But then I remember being grateful that I didn't make any reservations for us to go eat somewhere afterward."

Don, Mitch and Debbie nod in silence as they absorb Kevin's story. Their silence is unexpectedly interrupted by a deep throat clearing. They all knew it was Mr. Perkins, the chief accountant with the firm and their boss.

"Okay, people. It's time you get back to your desks and get to work. The work is not going to take care of itself," he says.

They nod and begin walking past their boss. Mr. Perkins stops Kevin.

"Ah, Kevin. That was quite a story," he says.

"Thanks, Mister Perkins," the employee responds. "I didn't realize you were listening."

"I didn't mean to, but then I heard 'hot blond' and 'ropes' and 'fun-loving' and wanted to see where you were going with this," says Mr. Perkins. "Tell me, Kevin, how long have you been with this firm now?"

"It was a little over four years last month," Kevin answers.

"Well, I have been keeping an eye on you and I must say I have been impressed with your work. Let's have lunch today and talk about the possibility of assistant chief of accounting," says the boss. He gives Kevin a quick pat on the back and walks away.

"Yes sir!" Kevin beams.

Narrator
One of the mysteries of life is how two seemingly inconsequential events can be connected. In this case, it is the

failed attempt at bungee jumping and Kevin's possible long-awaited promotion. More to the point, it is Kevin's great story that may have been all Mr. Perkins needed to hear to help him decide to make this young man assistant chief.

In Defense of Yodeling

One aspect of life that seems to generate more than its share of mockery is yodeling. Even though it is not very popular now, yodeling still seems to be on the receiving end of wise cracks and borderline scorn. While I am not a particular fan of yodeling, I think it is high time we give this unique form of singing a break. Did you know, for instance, that the famous Tarzan yell is viewed as being a yodel-like call? In his original books on Tarzan, creator and author Edgar Rice Burroughs described this noise as, "the victory cry of the bull ape." That's cool. Who knew bull apes even have a victory cry? Does this mean they also have a victory dance? Did Tarzan do that, too? If so, did he ever dance with a bull ape? And if he did, does the universal rule of boys-lead and girls-follow apply when one dances with another that is outside their species? What else did Burroughs not tell us about?

Generally, many associate yodeling with Switzerland. Apparently, early Alpine shepherds started doing it as a way of rounding up cattle and communicating with others across the Alps. Interestingly, according to Wikipedia, the Roman emperor Julian, as far back as the fourth century, complained to his minions about some kind of shrieking noise coming from northern mountain people. After all these years, I find it interesting that being the first prominent critic of yodeling may be the one thing for which we remember Julian. Would he be pleased? Perhaps the only thing more trivial – in a negative way – would be for us to remember Julian as being the first prominent person to praise yodeling.

Even Thomas Edison ventured into the yodeling bubble. One of his first recordings was of yodeler L.W. Lipp. One observer – and I wish it had been me – wondered if this experience inspired Edison to refine his electric chair. (Come to think of it, that may be a tad harsh.) Since then, yodeling has had its ups and downs in the realm of pop culture. Artists ranging from Jimmie Rodgers and Miriam Makeba to The Kingston Trio and Jewel have tried their hand at yodeling with various degrees of success.

Occasionally, yodeling is heard and experienced here in the United States, but it remains more popular outside our borders. I will leave it to others to decide whether that is good or bad. Perhaps one way to surpass its previous heyday would be for America's first yodeling mime artist to step into the spotlight. In fact, it would be great if this artist – following a few successful television appearances – would put out a "live" album. It would not have to be taken from one individual performance. Rather, it could be a compilation of show-stopping performances at major venues throughout the country. I can "hear" the CD now: an initial burst of applause and screams when the artist first walks out on stage. This is followed by approximately five minutes of silence (the estimated length of the opening number) and then more applause when it is completed; more silence followed by applause; more silence & applause; and so on for about seventy-five minutes. In today's market, however, the artist would still have to promote the CD pretty heavily. (I recommend he avoid radio.) We could be talking monster hit here. Even more importantly, we could be talking a rebirth of a specific style of singing that would ensure its popularity for generations to come. Or not.

Another Cat Story

Lots of my friends have pets and they are always telling me stories of what funny things their cats or hamsters do. Mister Purr does funny things, too. I think they are a lot funnier than anyone else's pet, of course. Like the time I walked into my bedroom and found Mister Purr with my underwear on his head. That was so cute. I still don't know how he got into my dresser drawer but that doesn't matter. It was another smile given to me by Mister Purr.

But Mister Purr has a serious side, too. It's a side of him that he does not show to many others. But I think because the two of us are so close, he does not mind letting me see all of him. That is one of the many things about my life I am grateful for.

Mister Purr is a great protector. He is a serious protector. I remember a time when we were having mice problems in our house. There was some construction going on in the neighborhood and the workers must have stirred up a nest of some sort. It wasn't just our house either. The houses right around us were having mice problems, too. It seemed like a day didn't go by when we didn't see at least several mice scampering across our living room and kitchen. We called the exterminator but other than set out some traps, they didn't seem to help us all that much. It even got to be really frustrating for my husband. He said the city lights – the red ones – of all things help him relax so he started going downtown a bit more often than before. I must say going down there did seem to help his disposition.

But this is not about him. It's about Mister Purr and those nasty mice. When the mice first arrived I thought Mister Purr – being a cat – would leap into action right away and do what cats do. But that's not what Mister Purr did. At first I just thought he was being lazy. But one day I went down to our basement to do laundry when I heard this squeaking noise coming from the back corner. I was a little nervous but I decided to see what I could find out, so I slowly walked over to where the sound was coming from. There, dangling in front of me, was a mouse. It was hanging by its tail from one of the pipes running along the ceiling. Someone had tied a string to its tail and then the other end of the string to the pipe.

"What in the world," I remember saying out loud, even though no one was there.

The mouse was alive but I could see scratch marks and bruises on its face. I admit I was a somewhat unnerved by this. Who would do this? My husband? I sure did not want to touch that mouse even though I could see it was not having a good day. I hurried off to find my husband and ask him about it. He denied knowing anything about it, adding that was one less mouse we had to worry about.

The next day I returned to the laundry room to find not just that one mouse hanging by its tail but a second one right next to it. This was definitely more than a coincidence. By now that first mouse was dead. I could not help but wonder if these mice were being hung on purpose. After all, this sort of thing does not happen by accident. By the time there were six mice dangling by their tails I was sure of it. Something else I noticed was there were not any more mice running through other rooms in the house. In fact, there was no apparent sign of our having more mice problems at all. It was a miracle. Or was it?

I question that because the same day I saw those six mice hanging, I returned to the laundry room and saw Mister Purr perched atop the pipe from which the mice were hung. When I walked into the area, Mister Purr's head turned sharply. He stared directly at me. The last time I felt this level of intensity from him was on that airplane when he saved us from those terrorists. Our eyes remained locked on each other for what seemed like minutes. Then, without even a soft meow, Mister Purr turned back to what he actually seemed to be doing: examining the knots to ensure they were not loose. It was then I realized that Mister Purr was handling our mouse problem in his own special way.

Sure, he could have killed those mice in the way most cats do. But that would not have stopped the mice from coming into our house. They would have kept coming without realizing the danger that awaited them. But, by hanging up each intruder by their tails, Mister Purr was telling the mice to beware. In fact, he was telling them to stay away. This message definitely worked because we never had any mouse problems after that – even though the construction in our neighborhood continued. It seems as if mice do talk among themselves. And, even more than that, it seems Mister Purr talks even louder to them.

Life of Tie

Laughter erupted from the backroom. Also heard were the clinking of glasses and non-stop chatter. If one were to eavesdrop, they would be hard-pressed to exactly understand what was being said or by whom as those around the table kept talking over each other. But not in a negative or argumentative way. These were old friends enjoying their company, reliving happy memories and making new ones. It was a table where an outsider would want to be. Never mind they would not know anyone personally at the table. Never mind they might not be able to add to the conversation. Just being part of the uninhibited joy would be reason enough.

Around the table were old timers who had lived through rough patches, happy times and everything in between. They had seen good friends and not-so-good friends come and go. Yet, here these old timers were, not quite what they used to be but still possessed with spark and still with an interest in the future, theirs and that of everyone else. They were glad to be alive and grateful to be what they were.

At the far end of the table was Pencil, not quite as pointed as he used to be but still thin and ready for use at a moment's notice. Next to him was Rubber Band. As usual, he took up several seats. He was still full of stretch and – despite rumors to the contrary – not in danger of losing the elasticity that remained his most lovable attribute. Several seats away was Shoe Lace. She was still "a hot looker," in the words of pencil and others who knew her way-back-when. She was still ready for action and kept an upbeat demeanor even though she was no longer as popular as she once was. Next to her, as usual, was Rock Candy, the group's acknowledged leader. With his trademark gruff voice, to outsiders he seemed unfriendly and unapproachable. But even a casual observer would soon see the untruth of those two characteristics. Rock Candy had a big laugh that never failed to bring a smile to anyone's face. Finally, there was Paper Clip. Paper Clip was quieter than the others, yet very dependable; a good friend everyone agreed. Easy to be around and a comfort to have nearby because one was never sure when she would be needed.

As usual, Rubber Band was the most talkative. "I'll give you that. Cuff Link always looked good. But I knew from the beginning he was a flash-in-the-pan. How could something that much trouble to put on last for long?"

"I know. I know," pencil chimed in. "But he sure looked good... Hey, Shoe Lace, didn't you once have a thing for him?"

Everyone laughed.

"Stop it, Pencil. Don't even think about that," she laughed.

"Well, I wouldn't blame you. He was a good lookin' guy. Still is."

Shoe Lace acknowledged his comment with a nod.

"He's still around but mainly you see him at the bottom of dresser drawers," Pencil said, "reliving the past and hoping for an occasional black tie dinner."

"Oh please. You're breaking my heart," huffed Rock Candy. "At least people know who Cuff Links is and still use him. I walk down the street right now and hardly anyone even knows who the hell I am. It's like I've become a trivial pursuit question."

"Oh come on, old timer," said Rubber Band. "It's not that bad. You've done a lot of good. Besides, if people don't recognize you, then it's their loss."

"Yeah, Rock," Paper Clip said. "We know who you are. Always will, too."

Rock Candy sighed. "Thanks, Clipper."

Rock Candy gazed off away from the table and his friends as the others nursed their drinks. His beginning days went back to before the ninth century. It was either out of India or Iraq – even he could not remember any longer – when he first appeared, the result of recrystallization. For a while, he tried out the name Rock Sugar – an idea suggested by one of his early agents – but then he fired the agent and went back to Rock Candy, thinking it sounded better. The changing names seemed to correspond with his years of uncertainty when he was not sure what his purpose was: medicine or treat. At first, he was comfortable with helping Chinese heroin addicts deal with withdrawal symptoms, but then he went back to being a simple treat. Life has been pretty easy since then. People still enjoy his company, though not as often as before. Maybe one day he'll make a comeback, he mused.

"Hey, earth calling Rock Candy," came Pencil's voice. "You okay? We thought we lost you there."

They all laughed, including Rock Candy.

"I'll tell you who's been around a long time," Rubber Band spoke up. His companions looked at him in anticipation of his answer. "Tie. Tie's been around almost as long as you, Rock."

"Of course. Of course," said Pencil.

"That's right," agreed Rock Candy. "I remember his beginning days. Even though he was just getting started, we traveled many of the same circuits."

"I remember reading once that he and bow tie were a team for a while," said Shoe Lace.

"That's right," said Rock Candy. "It's quite a story. We better order another round of drinks for this one."

As drinks and chips are served, the group settles in as their historian, Rock Candy, begins his narrative:

"They were a great team. One of the best. In their day they were as popular as butter and knife, bacon and eggs and, yes, even bumper and car. It seems like only yesterday when these upstarts caught the eye of fashion bugs. Old timers recall first noticing them working under the name of "cravats". They were donned by Chinese and Roman soldiers as far back as the seventeenth century as a way of giving these men of battle a certain "look" or distinction. Not only did the early warriors do well in battle, but they also gained notoriety by their snappy garb that seemed to be made snappier by the addition of material around their necks.

"Yes, Tie and Bow Tie seemed to be on their way even though they still had not yet adopted the stage names we know today. The Thirty Year War was an exciting time for them. It was during those three decades (1618–1648) when they were just starting out. They were fresh, unknown and full of swagger. Sure, what emerged from this period of history and mayhem of non-stop fighting and slaughter were famine, disease, national bankruptcies and population declines. But also what happened was that Croatian mercenaries were seen wearing small knitted neckware or neckerchiefs. The French saw this and took a big liking to it. In fact, this began what historians interpret as a trend by the French toward the adaption of entities or actions that on the surface run counter to all logic (later to be known as the Jerry Lewis syndrome). Soon, all Europe started following the French lead. The result was Tie and Bow Tie were being seen everywhere: offices, fancy parties, fancier restaurants, at the theater and even at sporting events. Men liked wearing them and women liked looking at their men wearing them.

"Perhaps one could say Tie and Bow Tie were seen as mankind's rejection of uncivilized behavior as represented by war, and embracement of peace and civilized behavior. They even helped give men a particular flare that accented their superiority to all other living creatures. This was the gift of Tie and Bow Tie to humans – a gift they brought to their admirers and one their fans eagerly sought.

"Tie and Bow Tie were becoming so popular they even triggered spin-offs, lesser known showbiz novelty acts that included bandannas and scarves. This, of course, is not to belittle or criticize bandannas and scarves. After all, they, too, had their own set of followers that exist even to this day. But no one ever doubted that the seeds of their popularity were planted by tie and bow tie. A great example of this is the book *Neckcothitania*, a book published in the nineteenth century that featured instructions and illustrations on the proper way to cravats. On the heels of this popular text came the Industrial Revolution. Say what you will about this sixty year period (1860–1920), but it was here where Tie and Bow Tie enjoyed their greatest stretch of popularity. They were, to coin the phrase, "top of the heap," – symbols of style, good taste, maturity and refinement.

"By now, Tie and Bow Tie were permanent fixtures in society. Life was good. Shirts of all kind – button-down or not – wanted to be their friend, wanted to be seen with them in a range of settings and venues. The good times seemed as if they were going to last forever. Then, as we have seen all too often, reality with all its indifference and complete objectivity, stepped in. Perhaps it was the successful end of the Second World War that ushered in a free-wheeling attitude that gained momentum in the 1950s and 1960s. This was not apparent at first as ties introduced a new dimension: "the bold look". They were shorter, more colorful and wider – so wide they looked something like a bib. At first, this appeared to be one more step toward greater popularity. Ironically, as the end of WWII became more of a memory, it turned into more of last-grasp effort. Open shirts became more of "the look". Casual Fridays were introduced and suddenly men began taking on a more personal look in what were traditionally professional settings. Ties and bow ties were viewed as being clothes of necessity rather than choice."

At this point, Paper Clip raised up in her chair, interrupting Rock Candy's monologue.

"Yes, Clip," Rock Candy said, curious but also a bit annoyed.

"Well, what you are saying is all true but you simply cannot talk about Tie or even Bow Tie without mentioning Turtleneck," she said.

"Paper Clip is right!" Pencil chimed in. "We all know that Turtleneck is a cocky upstart, but he's part of this story, too. He has to be."

Rock Candy. "You're right. You're right. Thanks Clip."

Rock Candy took a sip from his drink.

"If you recall, Turtleneck started off innocently enough," he continued. "Mainly people who worked at sea deserve the credit – if you want to use that word – for Turtleneck. The sea can get awfully cold and wearing ties was not practical. The seamen tried scarves but even they did not work all that well. So, someone – I don't know who – came up with our, uh, friend, Turtleneck.

"Yeah, Turtleneck has been nipping at Tie's heels ever since. Not enough to do any real damage. But, if anything, to remind him that fame is fleeting and not be taken for granted. Still, Tie keeps hanging in there. If anything, Bow Tie more than Tie seems to have hit a rough patch. Fewer and fewer men are seen wearing him. I have even heard of yard sales where dozens and dozens of bow ties are sold cheap. It is sad. What was once a real sign of class seems to becoming an afterthought. Bow Tie has even tried making himself more accessible with the clip-on version of himself. But even that hasn't caught on all that well. Go figure.

"I don't see Tie and Bow Tie being all that much of a team any more – if they ever were. If anything, they probably allowed themselves to be lumped together as a way of hanging onto their popularity, but that didn't work for long. Even now, they seemed to have gone their separate ways except for being worn around a person's neck."

Rock Candy pauses and then raises his glass. "This is good stuff," he says.

His table mates concur.

Rubber Band speaks up. "Tie has an amazing story," he says. "Those beginning days were really something. Now, he's settled in, part of the old guard like the rest of us."

"I'll drink to that," Shoe Lace says raising her glass. The group clinked their glasses and honored the toast. "Now, where is that guy of ours?"

Almost as if it had been planned, there was a rustle of noise from the entrance way and there stood Tie.

"Hey everybody!" he called.

Each called out to their long-time friend. They exchanged high-fives and hugs and ordered more drinks. The reunion could now officially begin.

Marrying Jesus

Recently, an ancient fragment of papyrus was discovered that some have interpreted as suggesting that Jesus was married. On this material, there is writing – supposedly from Jesus – that contains the phrase "my wife" followed by the name "Mary". This was very interesting and, not surprisingly, generated a lot of attention. For myself, this changes nothing in terms of my own spirituality or beliefs. At best, if true, I see it as an interesting tidbit that makes for interesting conversation. For others, of course, it is a BFD. I can appreciate that. For Catholics, the belief that Jesus was a bachelor is the reason priests remain celibate and do not marry and that women, generally, play a lesser role in the running of the church. Thus, the perspective of Jesus-as-a-bachelor has been around for well over a thousand years. With the revelation that he may have been married and even had a disciple that was female, it definitely raises questions and options that up till now have only been whispered and examined as a remote possibility.

Still, other than all the talk that followed this discovery, nothing dramatic has happened. Of course, in all fairness to those who write the rules for Catholics and other denominations, until something else is discovered that authenticates the scribble on the papyrus, we will not be seeing priests getting hitched any time soon. Nor, I suspect, will we see the Pope hosting a Friday night mixer at the Vatican. In a way, that is too bad 'cause I imagine the cardinals and bishops attending such a gathering would be dolled up more than the women. (How could any woman, for instance, compete with the hats and robes those guys have?) Also, if men of the cloth were to dally with women, would they say, "Who's your father?" rather than "Who's your daddy?" as the rest of us guys do?

If Jesus did have a female disciple and she was either his wife or main squeeze, did this cause resentment or jealousy among the disciples who, as far as we know, did not have any romantic entanglements? Was it akin to the relationship Snow White had with the seven dwarves? She seemed to be like a den mother to them, whereas her interaction with the Prince was, uh, much different. I always wondered about that. After all, as manly men of the forest, those dwarves carried with them as many basic needs as the Prince. Surely, at least one of them must have tried to charm his way into the arms of Snow White whenever the Prince was away doing princely things. If that was the case, then I suspect Grumpy is the one who attempted to act on his amorous feelings. My assumption, however, is Snow White rejected his advances. Otherwise, why would he be so grumpy all the time? Further, if he was successful in his wooing of Snow White, then he would no doubt have changed his name to "Sneaky".

But I digress. As wonderful in all areas of manliness as the Prince no doubt was, there is no way he would be a match for Jesus. Thus, even if any of the other disciples may have tried to put the move on Mary, I do not believe she would stray from the Son of God. Practically-speaking, if she did fool around at all, there is no way Jesus would not know. Let's face it: one of the perks of being the Son of God is there is very little going on that you do not know about. But, all that aside, suppose Jesus and this woman Mary were married. Can you imagine the pressure Mary must have been under trying to be the "perfect wife?" Forget it. On the surface, being married to someone who is perfect may seem like a dream come true, but in reality it has to be a massive burden. If something goes wrong in the house, whose fault is it? If there is an argument, who's going to win? For that matter, who started it? Being married to Jesus would be like the Washington Generals marrying the Harlem Globetrotters or Wiley coyote marrying the Road Runner. In each case, there is no doubt which one is the junior partner and which one is the senior partner.

And what would it be like if they had children? What would it be like having Jesus as a dad? At first, it would probably be pretty cool, especially when your dad would kick back and tell you stories of his early years and adventures. But suppose the son did not want to go into the family business? Or what kind of unique challenges would the daughter have trying to find a young suitor willing to marry into THAT family?

For both the wife and the kids, I see therapy very much as part of their routine. And forget about couple's therapy for the wife. What kind of insight would any counselor have that would make Jesus rub his chin and say, "Gee, I never thought of that." Nor can I imagine a counselor saying to Mary and Jesus:

Counselor: "Okay, our time for the day is nearly up, but this is what I want you two to work on between now and next week: Mary, tell Jesus what you are feeling every time you think he is correcting you. Remember, use your 'I' messages. He will understand."

Mary: "Of course he will understand. He always understands. He understands everything."

Counselor: "Now, Mary. We've talked about this. He's the son of God. He knows what you are experiencing and thinking and feeling, so he'll be onboard with what you share with him. He's a good man."

Jesus: "Good?"

Counselor: "I'm sorry. I meant to say 'perfect'."

Mary: "That's what I'm talking about. I get this all the time from the girls in the knitting club. 'Oh that man of yours is sooo perfect. You are soooo blessed.' It drives me crazy. I get blessed all day and all night. When do I get to bless him? Or anybody for that matter?"

Jesus: "Dear, remember last night our son sneezed and you blessed him."

Mary: "Oh, great. That's right. But you know what, somehow that's not the same thing... Jesus."

Jesus: "I'm right here."

Mary: "No, I didn't mean you."

Jesus: "But you said my name."

Mary: "Forget it."

Mary stands and storms out of the counselor's office. The counselor and Jesus look at each other for a few moments.

Counselor: "Women. Go figure."

Jesus: "I know. I already have."

Counselor: "Oh, right. Well, once again, thank you. You are always so insightful."

Jesus shrugs. The counselor moves toward the door but notices Jesus is not moving with him.

Counselor: "Jesus? Is everything okay?"

Jesus: "Sure, why wouldn't it be?"

Counselor: "Of course. But you seem troubled."

Jesus: "Well, it's my father... Do you have a few more minutes?"

The Joy of Twitter

In this day of social media, it is always a big deal when a celebrity announces they are starting a twitter account. Such news always fires up the base. It immediately sets us non-celebrities to thinking: "I will be able to talk with them directly, we'll get to know each other, meet for lunch, hang out and become best friends. This is gonna be great! I'm tired of hanging out with Slackjaw Blevins anyway. Sure, we grew up together and have been best friends since second grade. But Slackjaw is kind of a jerk and he never has anything new to say."

Suppose, for example, if Tony Stark, better known to all of us in the Free World and probably not-so-Free World as Iron Man, started a twitter account? As newsworthy such a turn of event might be, to this day, it has never been proved that communicating with a celebrity via twitter is a sure path to anything good. Take this exchange between Iron Man and one of his admirers:

@ Tony Stark
Hey. It's Tony Stark. What's goin on?
@ Top Fan#1
Tony! I can't believe we're talkin!
@ Tony Stark

It's true. Tell me about yourself.
@ Top Fan#1
Big fan, Tony. I live nearby.
@ Top Fan#1
Can I call you Iron Man?
@ Tony Stark
Sure, but I prefer Tony or Mr. Stark.
@ Top Fan#1
You bet. Talking with Iron Man is so cool.
@ Tony Stark
Call me Tony.
@Top Fan#1
Sure, but I wanna go with Iron Man.
@ Tony Stark
Come on, man. Go with Tony.
@Top Fan #1
Chicks must really dig Iron Man.
@ Tony Stark
Whatever.
@Top Fan#1
Does Pepper Potts have a sister?
@Tony Stark
None of your damn business.
@ Top Fan#1
Lighten up, Iron Man.
@Top Fan#1
Intro me to your lady friends.
@ Tony Stark
You're worse than the Mandarin.
@ Tony Stark

Stop writing me. We're not friends.

@ Top Fan#1

Screw you, man.

@ Tony Stark

I am no longer answering you.

@ Top Fan #1

Suit yourself, loser.

@ Tony Stark

You're the loser.

@ Top Fan#1

Shut up!

@ Tony Stark

No. You shut up!

What Could Go Wrong?

Throughout history there have been plenty of examples of decisions made by famous and non-famous people who were convinced beyond any doubt that they knew best in a particular situation. Given all the options at their disposal, the principle people involved believed the choice they made was beyond reproach and had little, if any, chance of turning out badly. While one might give them points for certainty, the wisdom of their conviction was another matter. Following are a few examples of misplaced certainty in-action:

Me

(I start this with me to demonstrate I, too, have gone down this path.) The year was 1964 and The Beatles were at the beginning stages of capturing the hearts of Americans and turning the pop music world upside down. As part of their incredible journey, a mini-tour of concerts was scheduled. One of the stops was to be at the Civic Center in Baltimore, approximately a twenty-five minute drive from my house. A few days before their appearance, one of my cousins called to say he was able to secure a number of tickets and asked if I wanted to go. I gave it some thought and decided that because The Beatles were new, they would be doing plenty of tours over the coming years, giving me a chance to see them in-person with little difficulty. So, I thanked my cousin for thinking of me and declined his generous invitation. The Beatles came to Baltimore and performed. Not only did they never return, this introductory tour turned out to be their only one. Ever. But at least I can claim I once saw Bobby Vinton perform in-person.

The Donner Party

James Reed was an ambitious man with visions of striking it rich in California. The year was 1846. Reed was putting together a small caravan to travel to the west coast from Springfield, Illinois. Looking ahead, he was confident such a journey, though not without challenge and some hardship, was not only doable, but not as difficult as people believed. Reed had just read a book boasting of a shortcut across the Great Basin that would lessen the trip by 350–400 miles and be on easier terrain. (Unbeknownst to the stars-in-his-eyes Reed, the author of this book had never actually taken this so-called short cut, so his claim was total speculation.) That aside, when looking at those prospects, what was there for Reed not to feel good about? In other words, what could go wrong?

Reed collected a number of travelers, including George and Jacob Donner, two brothers and their families. As they moved west, more people joined the travelers, reaching a total of eighty-seven. The group traveled in nine covered wagons. Along the way Reed came across an old friend who warned them not to take the new route he had originally intended as it was untested, unsafe and unfit for wagons. Reed ignored the advice. What followed was one disaster after another, including Native American conflict, injuries, horrible weather, disillusionment and tempers. What followed all that, in the words of one historian, was cannibalism, murder and bad behavior.

Even though this expedition has come to be known as the "Donner Party", I do not believe any of this episode was much of a party at all.

Husband: "Hey honey, we got an invitation from the Donners. They're having a party this Saturday. Let's go!"

Wife: "Sounds good. I'll call and see if we can bring anything."

Husband: "No. It says right here on the invitation that no one needs to bring any food. Wow. I guess they are providing all the goodies."

Imagine the surprised look on the faces of these and other invitees when the main party game is not duck-duck-goose, but something – shall we say – a bit more intense. I don't know about you, dear reader, but I plan to stick to those party games sponsored by Hasbro or Mattel.

Speaking of intense, I cannot imagine how tense it must have been for everyone as they sat around the campfire trying to stay alive, especially after a few of the travelers had already been eaten. Those poor people were starving, freezing and trying their damndest to not sneeze, cough or show any sign of physical weakness. The last thing any of them want to do is give Chef Donner an opening.

Donner: "Who sneezed? Was that you, Larry?"

Larry: "No. No. It wasn't me. It was Alice… Uh, I think Darren sneezed, too."

Darren: "Screw you, Larry. That wasn't me and you know it… Hey look. Stan's nose is running."

And on and on. The bad thing about cannibalism is that it often brings out the worst in people. It is almost like several people at the office that chip in and buy a bunch of lottery tickets. One of the tickets turns out to be the winning one and before you can say Goldman-Sachs, you have a bunch of people who only the day before were friends who enjoyed going to happy hour together, hanging out on weekends, etc. suddenly transformed into a pack of mad dogs. I think it is safe to say that if the members of the Donner Party had purchased a winning lottery ticket, none of them would have survived. What a tragedy that would have been: a winning ticket lottery that is not turned in.

Of the original group, forty-one died. One of the survivors, ironically, was the trip's organizer, Reed. During one of his moments of ill-temper, Reed actually stabbed one of his fellow travelers. In response, the group ordered Reed to leave. He and a companion went on ahead to California. They made it, but not without great struggle. To his credit, Reed, feeling guilty, helped organize rescue parties to try and save the remaining members of the party. Eventually, the survivors were found and brought back to California. It was then the legend of the so-called Donner Party began to take on a life of its own. Survivors began talking and/or writing about what happened to the point that what did happen became a story worthy of the Crypt Keeper. As for Reed, he reportedly enjoyed good fortune in California though you can bet it was no longer as a travel agent.

George Custer

Speaking of legends, there are few individuals of the nineteenth century that have remained part of the American landscape. One is Lt. Colonel George Armstrong Custer. Unfortunately for Custer, despite numerous biographies and even movies about him, his lasting reputation has been more minus than plus. This is largely the result of the judgment he showed at the Battle of Little Big Horn in June, 1876.

The American government was receiving numerous reports that American Indians were mobilizing like never before and that their intent was hostile. Custer and the approximately six hundred men in the Seventh Calvary under his command were one of several battalions involved in efforts to confront the hostile Indians in an effort to protect settlers and return the Indians back to their reservations. At one point, Custer received a word that an Indian encampment had been spotted. Custer then had the idea of launching a surprise attack against them. So far so good, except to do so would be to go against orders from his superior not to do that. At this point, he learned two things: his presence had been discovered by the Indians and that it was one of the largest gatherings of Indians any one had ever seen. Custer then made two other on-the-spot-decisions: to attack the Indians any way and to not take along any Gattling guns as he feared they would slow him down.

Custer: Men. I've called this meeting to amend the previous one about the surprise attack on the Indians.

Officer: "What is it, General? Are we calling off the attack?"

Custer: "No, we're still going to do it except it's not going to be a surprise any more. I'm told they know about us and possibly may even be preparing for a fight. Well, if it's a fight they want, then that's what we're going to give them. Let's go! Oh, one more thing, leave the Gattling guns here. Our own hand guns will do the trick."

Ah, out of the mouths of egocentric, megalomaniac babes. In the case of Custer and his men, what could go wrong? The answer can be summed up in one word: plenty! Soon afterward,

Custer led his men into armed conflict with the Indians. In less than an hour, he and the Seventh Calvary were no more. As it turned out, Custer finally got the national fame he longed for. Unfortunately, the price he paid for it did not include any press junkets, books, product endorsements, celebratory dinners or an autographed picture of himself in a fancy New York City restaurant.

(Author's note: At this point in this chapter following brief overviews of the Donner Party and Custer, I am thinking in comparison my decision not to go see the Beatles was not so bad.)

Movie Bad Guys

This observation has been made by others but I find it worth highlighting again because it fits so perfectly under the "What could go wrong?" premise. I, of course, am referring to movie bad guys. The scene is classic: the villain has the hero in his clutches and, in fact, is preparing to kill the good guy. Before doing that, of course, the villain must gloat and toss a few "nanny nanny boo boos" at the hero who, up to this point, has been a major thorn in the bad guy's side. Consequently, because of all the pent-up frustration and anger the bad guy has, he cannot help but taunt his arch enemy not unlike the way a house cat taunts a defenseless mouse. (Make no mistake, I am in no way defending this kind of behavior from the villain or the cat for that matter. Nevertheless, this is what they do. Another point, I understand there are those who adore their cats and often times for good reason. Still, every once in a while these cat lovers need to take off their rose-colored glasses and see that from time to time Fluffy or Mister Jingles can be a sadistic son-of-a-bitch. Granted, the cat may not have dreams of world domination like most movie bad guys, but is it necessary that they toy with the poor mouse before sending it to its great reward? And while I am on the subject, when this cruel cat and mouse dance is going on, do you think the mouse is at any point thinking, "Gee, maybe I've been all wrong about this cat?" or "Hey, I may get out of this after all." or "You know. I think the cat and I could actually become friends.")

So, the movie bad guy and the hero banter for a few minutes as things look increasingly grim for the hero. Finally, the hero, in a kind of "okay, you got me" gesture, seems to acknowledge his defeat and says something to the effect of: "Okay. Since I am going to die in the next few minutes, tell me of your plan to (fill-in-the-blank.)" Upon hearing these words, the bad guy practically explodes with delight. This is what he has been waiting for: a chance to brag about himself to the one person – his nemesis – who has been his primary hurdle. Such an opportunity, one could say, might even be considered to be cathartic. The bad guy then proceeds to outline in almost graphic detail what he plans to do and how, when and where he plans to do it. He does not mind being so open because he is certain the good guy is going to die in the next few moments. Following that, the bad guy invariably leaves the actual killing of his rival to his underlings so he can go begin the countdown, push the "go" button or do whatever needs to be done to begin the final phase of his dastardly plan. We all know what happens next. The good guys breaks free of his bonds, dispatches the underlings, foils the plot, kills the bad guy, blah blah blah.

One question I always have after watching this familiar scene play itself out is: why do all these evil geniuses have such inept underlings? The hero is either tied up or been beaten half-to-death, yet these henchmen still do not seem able to close the deal on this guy by killing him. I can only imagine how lax the search process must have been when the bad guy was interviewing for loyal sidekicks.

Cows and Stairs

There is an urban legend that has been making the rounds for a good while now. It pertains to cows and stairs. Specifically, there are those who contend cows are unable to walk down a flight of stairs. This is not true. They can. But what is true is they do not like it as it is an action that does not come easily to them. The primary reason for this is their knees. They do not bend properly. (For example, a horse can navigate stairs more easily because this animal's knees bend in a way that is more conducive to the challenge of dealing with steps. So, if you are ever asked to choose between escorting a horse or a cow down the Washington Monument, do not think twice. Go with the horse.)

Thinking about this interesting factoid got me to wondering about the poor guy who first discovered the problem cows have with stairs. I see it as another one of those "what could go wrong?" scenarios.

Guy: "Oh my God. It's my wife. Hurry. Hurry. Get dressed."

He scrambles around frantically trying to put his clothes on and make the bed at the same time.

Guy: "Hurry. She's almost inside. We need to get downstairs. Come on. Come on."

He stops suddenly in his tracks. His eyes are wide open.

Guy: "What? What do you mean you don't want to walk down the stairs? You're kidding. You've got to. We've got to. Come on sweetie, let's go."

The man, growing increasingly frantic, stops again.

Guy: "What do you mean going down steps frightens you? You're telling me this NOW! Oh, Jesus. I'm so screwed. Shit. Shit. Shit."

He turns to the bedroom door as he hears his wife's footsteps. The door opens. The silence is deafening as the man stares at his wife and she stares at him. She keeps looking back and forth between her husband and the cow.

Wife: "John. What is going on here? And who is that?"

Guy: "Hi, honey. It's great seeing you. Ah, this is Daisy. She's the, ah, new temp I was telling you about that we hired at the office."

Wife: "New temp? Then what is she doing in our bedroom? What's going on?"

Guy: "She was helping me try to find those papers for the Lonnegan case. You know. The Lonnegan case."

Wife: "I told you last night they were downstairs on the dining room table."

Guy: "Of course! I'm such an idiot. No wonder we couldn't find them here."

The wife stares hard at her husband. There is a great deal of exasperation and skepticism on her face. The man steps forward and takes his wife by the arm.

Guy: "Honey, could we step outside here for a second? Excuse us a moment, Daisy."

Wife: "What is it?"

The two step outside the bedroom into the hallway. He closes the door.

Wife: "What?"

Guy: "Ah, how would you feel about Daisy staying with us for a while? Maybe, uh, a good while. I'm thinking she could just live here in the bedroom."

Ever-Growing Grumpiness

Do men get grumpier as they age? Though there is probably not any scientific proof of this, I cannot help but think it is true. Never mind that I am growing older and becoming grumpier. Since it is happening to me, then it must be happening to everyone. Right? In my defense, being grumpier is just easier than the opposite. Let's be honest, being polite is a lot of work. For instance, it requires mustering up the energy to display good manners, be cordial, ask others about themselves and then actually listen to what they say, respond to questions they may have about you, etc. Before you know it, you are involved in actual conversation that might even lead to a friendship if things get too far out of hand. As I hobble into the grumpy phase of life, I have to ask myself: is that what I really want?

Every week or so I go by my local bank to conduct some type of transaction (as well as take several of the candy treats they set out). I walk through the door and silently growl at one of the signs they have posted that boasts how important customer service is to them. As I get closer and closer to the teller I find myself tensing up as I know whoever waits on me is going to be bursting with smiles, good cheer and, worst of all, small talk.

I always seem to get the one who is most upbeat. This fact seems to be one of life's little jokes that it keeps playing on me.

"Good morning, sir," he bellows. "How are you today?"

I purposely keep my answers short and to the point. "Fine," I say. I even keep the grin going with that answer tight and to the point.

"That's great," he says. "Just great."

At this point, I feel as if he is taunting me. Either that or he is oblivious to my attempt to get him to close his pie hole and just move along with my transaction.

"So, what are you up to today?" comes the next inevitable question.

I hate this question. Especially from him. I do not want him to know what I will be doing even if it is nothing. In fact, because I have no plans for the day except going to the bank makes me feel even grumpier than I already am and more miffed with this "chatty Cathy" of a teller. I also find myself trying not to make eye contact with this guy as I feel doing so only encourages his banter. But nothing I do seems to slow this guy down.

"I think there's supposed to be a good game on this afternoon," he says, ignoring the fact I never did answer his question about what my plans for the day were. I also notice he has kept his comment vague. By just using the word "game", he is leaving it to me to fill in that blank. Very clever. He probably has a response all lined up no matter what "game" or team I mention. At this point, I feel as if I must say something even if I honestly do not know about any alleged game that is set to happen later on.

"Is there?" I finally say, knowing full well that is such a lame response. (At this point, is it necessary that I mention this makes me feel even grumpier than I was moments before?)

"Yeah," he says. "It's supposed to be a good one, too."

The expression on my face right now is frozen. What to say? What to do? Where is this conversation going? What would happen if I just turned around and walked out of the bank? Fortunately, I am saved from having to respond to my own array of self-directed questions. Ironically, it is the teller himself who saves me.

"Okay, sir, is there anything else I can do for you?" he seems to grin more than actually say.

This, of course, is the precise opening I have been waiting for. "No, that'll do it," I say, gathering my bank book and slips of paper and turning toward the exit all in one fluid motion. It is a maneuver I have perfected and one I believe is worthy of the late Fred Astaire. As I walk toward the door I cannot help but wonder if this "kid" even knows who Fred Astaire was. But that thought is interrupted by that same "kid's" voice to the next customer: "So, how are you today?" I feel bad for the recipient of that question.

Postscript

I do not want to give the impression I am carrying a grudge against that particular bank teller. I am not. Perhaps if we were to meet in some alternative universe, we would be the best of buds. Until that day comes along, however, I will remain content to keep things between him and me as they are. Not too long ago, I was in a restaurant when our waitress bounced over to welcome us and officially begin the "get-them-what-they-want-to-eat" process. It was almost as if she had popped out of a birthday cake.

"Hello there. And how are you today?" she beamed.

Already I could feel myself sinking back down into my seat. I will not bore you any more than I probably am with a breakdown of our conversation and her over-the-top exuberance. Suffice to say, I found it off-putting. But in all fairness to her and the bank teller, I concede my reaction to them speaks to my own evolution into a first-rate grump. I take no pride in the fact these two individuals were simply trying to be nice while I was being a real fuddy-duddy. But sometimes, I believe being at least a tad grumpy serves a purpose, too, even if it is not of the full-blown old man grumpy variety. Since none of us are like squid which emit a black ink-like substance in self-defense, perhaps being grumpy is a good way to go – even for those who upon first sight do not seem as if they need it.

****

The President of the United States walks back into the Oval Office. It had been a long day, but a good day, too. His speech before the General Assembly of the United Nations had gone well. The signing ceremony with his Soviet counterpart putting into place the arms reduction agreement served as a strong complement to his goal of making the world safer for everyone. He stood gazing out the window and reflected on the long-term significance of the day. Suddenly, the voice of his trusted secretary, Marge, could be heard over the intercom.

"I'm sorry to disturb you, Mister President," she said. "It's your mother on line two."

"Thanks, Marge," the President said. He sighed and pushed down on line two. "Hello, Mom, how are you?"

"Hello, Raymond. This is your mother."

"I know, Mom. How are you? Did you hear my speech?"

"Never mind me, Raymond. And never mind that speech even though it was too long. I'm calling about your Uncle Carl."

"Uncle Carl. What's wrong? Is he okay?"

"No, he's not, Raymond. You know how sensitive he is. His feelings are hurt. Yesterday was his birthday and you didn't call him to wish him a happy birthday."

"Well, Mom. If you've been following the news, I've been kind of busy lately. Between that arms treaty and the speech and the budget talks with Congress, my plate has been pretty full."

"You know how Uncle Carl loves you, Raymond. You couldn't pick up the phone and call him? I'm talking five minutes, Raymond. Just five minutes."

"Oh come on, Mom. It's not like I did it on purpose."

"You're a good boy, Raymond, but you should have called your Uncle Carl. That's all I'm saying."

"Okay. Okay. I'll call him now. I'm sorry"

"That would be good, Raymond, even though you'll be a day late. I'm sure he'll forgive you."

"Ok, Mom. Thanks. I'll call him now."

"Thank you, Raymond. And don't forget your cousin Cece's anniversary is next week."

Another Postscript

To return to my original point, it is so much easier being a grump. You let loose with whatever is on your mind with little regard to whom or what you might offend and the reaction – at least from family – is tolerance (or is it endurance?). Either way, this is one of the many advantages of entering into the winter of one's life. One of the burdens of youth is often having to do the heavy lifting when it comes to relationships. As we see from the above scene, it is the young or younger, no matter their station in life, who get nagged for not having called their grandparents in two weeks, for not remembering their Aunt Lillian's seventy fourth birthday, or for being the one who has to sit next to Grandpa Mike at Thanksgiving. God bless those younger than me. Now excuse me while I go tell those pesky kids to get off my lawn.

Theodore Roosevelt, Librarian

Poll after poll show that many historians and lay people agree that of all of America's presidents, the greatest was Abraham Lincoln. Lincoln was the 16th president of the U.S. and the first Republican commander-in-chief. He, of course, led the country through its greatest crisis – a civil war in which the unity of the entire nation was at stake. That the country remained united following the civil conflict is in no small way a tribute to the strength and wisdom of Lincoln. As we all know, over the years many books have been written about this unique man. In fact, this total (which approximates over fifteen thousand) is greater than the combined number of books written about Donald Trump, Bea Arthur, Larry Holmes, the entire Radio City Music Hall Rockettes, and the city of Akron, Ohio.

Recently, a new book about Lincoln was released depicting his years before being elected to the presidency in 1861. This one was unlike any other Lincoln book before it. In it, the author outlines Lincoln's adventures as a vampire hunter. To add further credence to this, a movie was made based on the book. If having a book and movie come out about a particular topic does not make it true, then I do not know what would. Perhaps a mini-series on any major cable network would erase doubts some skeptics might have. Either way, it is good enough for me, so I say 'to hell' to any non-believers. People like that probably don't believe Marilyn Quayle and Tokyo Rose were really the same person either.

This new insight into Lincoln's past is a true revelation. It is my hope it will serve as the beginning of a new wave of historical output about our nation's other presidents. For instance, will we soon learn that President Washington was also a werewolf watcher, that Andrew Jackson was captain of a synchronized swim team, that James Polk collected unicorns, that Herbert Hoover was one of the original members of the Harmonicats, that Dwight Eisenhower was a hand model, or that Ronald Reagan was an actor? I know. I know. All this sounds preposterous. But I am certain the same reaction was heard about Lincoln and vampire hunting until both a book and movie about it came out. Who's laughing now?

Though in no way do I or would I consider myself a historian, the Lincoln revelation inspired me to conduct my own research on one former president I have always found to be of interest. I speak of Theodore Roosevelt, who stepped into the role in April 1901, following the assassination of William McKinley. I always viewed Roosevelt to be a dynamic and powerhouse of a public figure in multiple ways. Though my research revealed little to make me doubt that observation, I was still very surprised to learn that in his early years Roosevelt, much like Lincoln, had what can only be termed as "other interests". I speak of the four years Roosevelt spent in his early teens as a librarian. That's right. We are talking about Theodore Roosevelt: Librarian.

Unlike me, TR was born into wealth in October, 1858. He was raised in New York City, a growing urban sprawl that was beginning to take on all the characteristics we know today: tall buildings, pot holes, extensive culture, and the fact it never ceases to sleep. TR, however, slept. He was a rather sickly child who was home-schooled by his parents. In fact, because of his asthmatic problems, Teddy often had to sleep propped up in a chair. The parents did not want to risk making their child even sicker than he always seemed to be. They knew what they were doing, as one result of their caution was that TR grew older – as did many children back then and, even today, children tend to do.

It was when he was in his early teens that TR started to feel his oats as a budding young man even while being watched over closely by Mom and Dad and their servants. Despite his bouts of ill health, young Teddy had a mischievous side that foreshadowed the often hyperactivity for which he became known as an adult. No question, this kind of 'push me pull me' dynamic weighed heavily on TR who liked pressing his face against the window and watching life pass him by less and less. More and more, he saw himself as a person of action. Being disengaged from the adventures of the world was not how he saw himself.

Drawing from my heavy "research" on this topic, I now wish to present two things: (1) what is called on television a "reenactment" of young Roosevelt's early teen years that led to his time as a librarian; and (2) testimonials from those who knew TR and his family back then. (I should note that none of these people have ever been interviewed before primarily because they never existed. That small detail aside, I found their insight and perspectives to be quite enlightening. Without them, young Roosevelt's years as a librarian would remain unknown much like the humor in every damn one of Pauly Shore's movies. Let us begin.

Narrator

Teddy plopped down in the cushy living room chair, a look of frustration on his face. He could hear the voices of his parents coming from the drawing room. As usual, they were talking about him and, again, he did not like what he was hearing.

"It is time we got Teddy more out on his own. Out of the house, so he can make more of a mark on the world," said his father, the man for whom young Teddy was named.

"I agree, dear, but we don't want to push him too hard," said his mother.

Theodore Roosevelt, Sr. and Martha "Mittie" Bulloch had been married since 1853. Their coupling resulted in four children: Anna, born in 1855, Teddy in 1858, Elliot in 1860, and Corinne in 1861. Generally, it was a happy unit though not without its fair share of challenges. The mother, "Mittie" as she was known, had her share of health issues. The result was that Anna, as she aged, assumed a number of the parenting responsibilities that normally would have fallen to the mother. Anna helped ensure her siblings carried out their duties, provided back-up to the father, and served as the go-to person for Teddy, Elliot and Corrine whenever they needed approval and someone to talk with about matters that might be troubling them. In fact, Anna continued to serve in this capacity with Teddy well into each of their adult years.

Colin "Cussie" Myers. *("Cussie" was the Roosevelt's stable master for many years. He was first hired by TR's father and stayed with them until two years after young Teddy was elected* governor of New York in 1898. The four Roosevelt children loved "Cussie" as he would give them rides on some of the family's prized horses. However, his departure from the family was not without controversy. "Cussie" was believed to be involved in the illegal trafficking of hamsters in the black market. To those close to TR, none were surprised he never mentioned "Cussie" in any of his writings or speeches in his later years.)

"I know Teddy always believed his parents held him back. At times he would talk to me about how he wanted to leave home and make a name for himself and be his own person. For a while, he even considered taking on a new name, Lesley Duvall. Looking back, it's probably a good thing he stuck with his own name."

This particular conversation between TR's parents is noteworthy because it set in motion the beginning of the young boy's adventures outside the house. Specifically, it led to his librarian years. According to witnesses inside the house, after listening to his parents talk, TR actually interrupted their private talk to plead his case for being more "like everyone else." This was a bold move on TR's part as challenging his parents was something he or any of the Roosevelt children rarely did.

Miss Betsy. *(Betsy was the Roosevelt's chief maid. At the time Mrs. Roosevelt hired her, Betsy was already in her mid-sixties and beginning to slow down in terms of how much work she could get done during the course of day. This fact led to the Roosevelt's hiring a team of housekeepers to assist Betsy in her duties. As the head housekeeper, Betsy supervised the other house workers. She enjoyed having authority over others so much that, according to one witness who refused to go on the record with this account, one day Betsy and TR's father got into a heated argument over which Adams – John or John Quincy – was the worse president. At one point, Betsy reportedly slapped the father. According to the same witness, TR Senior later thanked Betsy for the slap.)*

"I was so proud of Teddy that day he stood up to his folks. They was surprised but he held his ground and told 'em he was ready. Ready to break free."

Narrator

TR and his parents indeed had a long talk that day in which they shared many things. For instance, the father confessed to one day wanting to begin a professional league of thumb wrestlers. In between coughs, the mother said it was her dream to live out the remainder of the week. (She actually did more than that. "Mittie" lived till 1884. She died at the age of forty-eight.) Teddy, however, said he wanted to make a difference in the world: be a leader so he could direct others in a way that would better their lives. Though no concrete decision came out of this family discussion, father, mother and son seemed to have developed a tighter bond as a result of it. Several weeks after the discussion, the father came home one day very excited. He called everyone, including Anna, Elliot and Corrine, into the drawing room.

Miss Betsy. "The Mister seemed very excited. We all gathered round him waiting for him to catch his breath. I noticed both his thumbs was bandaged. I'm sure the others saw that, too, but no one said anything. Finally, he spoke up and said earlier in the day he was told of a position opened at the local library. It was for assistant librarian or something like that. Everyone looked at young Teddy 'cause by then we all knew this kind of position was what he was hoping for. I could tell he was excited. His face got all red and that was always a sign."

Tommy Elkins. *(Tommy was one of the boys in the neighborhood and one of Teddy's playmates. Teddy was shy except when he was around TR. TR seemed to bring out the playful side of him.)*

Tommy. "I remember Teddy came to see me one day. That was unusual because I don't recall him leaving the house much. Usually I would go over to him. But this day was different. He was very excited. He started telling me about the job at the library. Even though he hadn't started it, Teddy knew he would like it. But he also knew it was not something he would always want to do. But, boy, he had ideas even then that he wanted to start at the library. Teddy always loved to read and wanted others to, too, even though he knew there were those who had trouble with that. He said he would start a reading group and call it 'Teddy Roosevelt and the Rough Readers.' I thought it was a great idea but I wasn't sure how those at the library would take to it."

Narrator

According to rumors, those at the library at first were reluctant to hire TR. While they found him to be likeable enough, it was clear he was inexperienced and not well versed in administrative work, did not know the library's own internal system, or knew much about managing others. One employee, Ida Cove, talked of TR's beginning days at the library.

Ida Cove. "Teddy was kinda over his head at first. Oh, he was smart enough and had a lot of enthusiasm but he didn't know how we did things. I felt sorry for him. But I also felt sorry for Mr. Whitlock, our head librarian. He was not the most patient of men, but neither was Teddy. But Mr. Whitlock worked hard with Teddy because he was good friends with his father. I sometimes think if Mr. Whitlock had to do it over again he would not have agreed to hire Teddy. Teddy was a handful." (*Editor's note: An interview with Mr. Whitlock had been scheduled but his tragic death caused us to cancel the sit-down session with him. The cause of his death remains unknown though authorities report his body was found riddled with bullets.)*

Narrator

TR took the job of assistant librarian shortly after his thirteenth birthday. This library at the time contained well in excess of three thousand books, ranging from non-fiction, biographies and books on science to ones on philosophy, autobiographies, instructional manuals and novels. Among the most popular books were *Shoeing a Horse for Dummies, Twenty-Five Shades of Gray,* Betty White's autobiography *My Early Years,* and *Huck Finn and the Temple of Doom,* Mark Twain's lesser known sequel to *Huck Finn.*

Ida Cove. "No doubt Teddy wanted to leave his mark on the library. Make a difference. One of the first things he did was organize his Rough Readers group. He did it without Mr. Whitlock's permission. When Mr. Whitlock found out he was angry. He didn't want anyone being singled out because they had trouble reading. He protested to Teddy who would not back down. Mr. Whitlock was very exasperated. He said Teddy had the stubborn streak of a bull and the brains of a moose. When Teddy found out what Mr. Whitlock had said, he got a real determined look on his face and said he would never forget that for as long as he lived."

Narrator

Membership into TR's rough readers group was surprisingly high. This was helped by the ambitious young man's enthusiasm for what he called "bagging" new recruits.

Andrew Laycock. *(Andrew was one of the charter members of the Rough Readers group. At the time, he was a young boy, not even in his teens. Even though he could not read very well, he frequented the library as it was a sanctuary from a household where his parents – both music lovers – hosted jam sessions each day for members of the local Accordion Appreciation Society.)*

Andrew. "Teddy was always so persuasive and he seemed so much fun. He knew I couldn't read all that well but didn't seem to mind. After a while, I stopped being much concerned about it, too. In fact, I don't consider myself to being much of a reader even now. But that's okay. Teddy came up with this idea for us to get more people to join our group. At one point he said we should go out and bag a few people and maybe even mount them on the walls of the library. I and a couple of others thought that was so funny. But I remember when Teddy first suggested it, he was the only who wasn't laughing."

Narrator

By now TR was entering into his third year as assistant librarian. Mr. Whitlock's confidence in his young assistant seemed to have grown as he was spending less time behind the front desk with TR and more time in his office with the door shut.

TR's enthusiasm seemed to grow in direct proportion to the freedom Mr. Whitlock gave him.

Ida. "At one point, Teddy came up with this new classification system for our books that reminded me of the Dewey Decimal System that didn't come out for another several years after what Teddy came up with. (*Editor's note: The Dewey Decimal System, a library classification system, was created in 1876 by Melvil Dewey. The system revolves around a number of classifications based on various subjects, including history, biology and geography, philosophy and psychology, religion, and the arts.*) Teddy had his own categories such as plants and buffalo and foreign countries. It helped keep all the books straight though I'm not sure by how much. Every time someone would bring in a new member to the Rough Readers group or go to check out a book on their own, Teddy would give out with one of his 'Bully!' cries. He sure did liven things up."

Narrator

But these years as a librarian were not all smooth or without incident. As was the case at all libraries, there was a problem with overdue books. Some of the members of the library checked out books but failed to return them on time. These infractions brought out TR's dark side, an aspect of himself he did not like others to see. Whenever he became angry, TR, even then, was not one to sit still. It was as if his temper took hold of him and drove him to act in ways even he would think twice about under other circumstances. One particular member of the library, a young man named Stan Juan, was the library's most flagrant violator of its return policies. One time Stan had a book out that was over six months overdue. With each passing day, those who worked at the library could see the agitation over this within TR grow.

Ida. "I was usually the one who brought Teddy the weekly report on the status of books that were currently checked out. It got to a point when the only name Teddy looked for on the list was Stan's. Teddy would see Stan's name and pound his fist on the front desk. No question he was upset. We didn't know what to do or what Teddy was going to do. But we sure found out. Shortly after the sixth month of Stan's book being overdue, Teddy let out with a, "That's the last straw!" Everyone in the whole library heard it."

Andrew. "We had a meeting of the rough readers group later the same day that Stan's bill was six months overdue. Teddy was usually very jovial during those times but he wasn't at that meeting. We could all tell something was troubling him. Finally, Teddy interrupted our 'old business' portion of the agenda and said he had something to talk about. Something he said he needed our help on. He really got our attention when he said that.

"You have to remember, up till then Teddy had done nothing but help all of us. He identified each and every one of us in the group as people who had trouble reading. We would meet and talk about our trouble with words or not being interested in reading. It really brought us together so none of us felt as if we were alone. It didn't even matter that Teddy never helped any of us read better. We just enjoyed coming to the library and having each other for friends. And Teddy did that. So, when he said he needed our help, we were all ears. Even "Big Ears" Wallace who was part of the group. He had a small head and big ears so he really did seem like he was all ears. Even he listened extra hard."

Narrator

At that meeting, TR told the group it was time to show Stan Juan that he could no longer thumb his nose at the rules of the library. He said that if the library was going to continue to be seen as a beacon for all other libraries and the city of New York, then it was time for them to confront Stan Juan with his bill. Stan, he said, had to be made an example to all other violators. All seventeen members of the rough readers group agreed to support TR and his plan – before he even said what it was. TR described his plan as simple yet direct, and guaranteed it would settle this issue "once and for all." Still, without telling the members what he was going to do, TR produced the library record book from his coat pocket, waved it in the air and called out "Follow me!" With that, the group rose as one and followed TR out of the library.

"We're going to Stan's house, men," Teddy said. "We are going directly to the violator himself."

Fortunately, young Stan lived less than a dozen blocks away from the library, so the group's charge was not as long as it could have been. Due in large measure to Teddy's energy and encouragement, with each passing block the group seemed to escalate its pace. Pedestrians on the street stepped aside for the group. Women lifted their young children into their arms for fear of watching the fired-up group knock down their son or daughter. Even grown men seemed taken aback by TR and his followers. But no one tried to intervene. At the first sighting of Stan Juan's house, the group stopped almost as one. The imposing house sat atop a hill. TR let them collect their thoughts.

"There he is, my friends," TR said. "He is calm in his false security. We will disrupt his calm and right this wrong. We will make him pay what he owes the library we love! We will make him pay his fine and with interest."

With that, the group members let out with a roar as TR's call of "Charge!" could be heard over their voices. What followed quickly became part of TR's legend. It was talked about for years by those who participated in the charge, by those who witnessed it, by those who heard about it, and by those who claimed to be part of it but in reality were not. Collectively, they spoke of the day when Teddy Roosevelt and his Rough Readers charged up Stan's Juan's hill.

Andrew. "I look back on that day now and really think we made history. We all felt so proud of ourselves and of Teddy, too. Some people said we may have over reacted, but we all felt we were doing the right thing."

Narrator

The charge was a high point of TR's time as a librarian. To this day, historians debate how that time may have influenced TR's years as a soldier, an elected official, including his time as president, in public service and as an international figure. For instance, in their discussions and writings they have sought to parallel the creation of the rough readers and the attempt by TR and this group to charge-up Stan's Juan's hill with his adventures in the military. No direct link has been made but each year seems to produce more insight and meaningful interpretation.

Less than a year after Stan's one bill incident, TR resigned his position from the library. He claimed he had done all he could and it was time to move on. His announcement seemed to correspond with Mr. Whitlock coming out of his office and once again working the front desk. Again, no connection between the two has been made. As TR moved on with his life and career, he rarely talked about his library years. Perhaps he was too modest. Perhaps, in retrospect, he felt it paled in comparison to his time in the military, his tenure as governor, vice president or president, his world travels, or his Nobel Peace Prize. But, perhaps it was the reality that the famous charge made by him and his rough readers on Stan's one bill was a failure. When TR and his followers reached the door to Stan's house, much to their disappointment they found no one home. They pounded on every door to the house they could fine. They peaked in every window they could. Their efforts all came to nothing. It turns out Stan and his family were out of town on a brief holiday. Shortly after returning, they quietly paid the overdue fine. Stan continued to frequent the library and continued to not return books on time. No one knows what became of Stan other than he became a small part in the legend that became Theodore Roosevelt.

Unsung Heroes

Never before in the history of mankind have we as a human race been more civilized. (Granted, never before have more people on the planet been killed due to our own aggressive inclinations, lax attitude toward violence, craving for power, and prioritization of profit over human life. But never mind all that.) The point is: How many cable television subscribers were there in the eighteenth century? How many members of the Roman Senate had heated toilet seats? How many choices of mouth wash did the ancient Mayans have? How many different flavors of Coca Cola did the revolutionaries at Valley Forge have? How many dishwashers did those who lived during the Ming Dynasty have? How many self-checkout lines were there at the local grocery store in downtown Stalingrad? In other words, today we are bursting at the seams with examples of our cushy lives that make us look like Gods compared to those who came before us. (Granted, there are millions of people throughout the world today going to bed each night without food, water or shelter. And granted the air we breathe is becoming increasingly unsafe. But never mind all that.) Let us not forget we humans remain on top of the food chain of planet Earth and never before has that position been more secure.

Without question, all the luxuries we enjoy are great. Even though puppies are cuter, tigers braver, manatees more patient, chimpanzees more loyal and peacocks more majestic, can we all agree that being human is pretty darn cool? How many other living creatures have fun things like senior proms, monster movies, senior citizen discounts, coffee tables, hot air balloons, remote control or socks that do not need to be held up with garter belts or rubber bands? Yet with all that we have and do not really need, it is important for us to every so often take time to recognize the unsung heroes that either contributed to or inspired the creation of our multitude of creature comforts. Without them, we would be the lesser for it and probably be reduced to spending more time not sitting in our favorite chair in the den, not waiting until the shower water is not-too-hot or not-too-cold before stepping under it, or not staying up quite so late getting to the next round of our favorite video game.

In no particular order (because they are all important) is a list of some of the more noteworthy unsung heroes that have helped give us such great lives:

* Cicadas – These creatures pop out of the ground once every seventeen years and live for only several weeks. As a result, time is of the essence to them. If ever there was a creature that wants to move things along, it is the cicada. So, thank you cicadas for being the inspiration behind instant coffee and speed-dating.

* Turkeys – It is said and has yet to be proved differently that no one turkey ever gobbles alone. One starts and within seconds they all chime in. If turkeys performed in Las Vegas, you can bet there would be no solo acts. So, thank you turkeys for being the

inspiration for barber shop quartets, glee clubs and quite possibly The Johnny Mann Singers.

 * Sharks – Does anyone ever tire of watching the promos for "Shark Week" when one of the great whites leaps out of the water baring all its pearly whites? I sure don't. Even though I have never watched one episode of "Shark Week," I sure do love those promos. I think of them every time I venture to the dentist and he asks me to open wide and say, "Aaaaaaahhhh." So, thank you sharks for helping me and so many others, I am sure, be better patients at the dentist.

 * Sloths – Over the years these unusual mammals have gained a reputation for being lazy. In fact, one of the so-called seven deadly sins is called "sloth". Since early Christian days, sloth has come to mean physical or even spiritual laziness. Sure, some scientists have found this creature, which dwells in rain forests in Central and South America and sleeps as much as eighteen hours per day, to be a source of fascination. Yes, it seems to spend the majority of its days hitting the snooze button. But does that make it lazy? I think not. If anything, this is a creature that is nothing if not focused. It knows how it is going to spend each and every one of its days. I wish I could say that. In that regard, it is not unlike another creature that has gained in numbers over the years: the couch potato. These creatures also require much sleep and rest each day. However, unlike the sloth, in order to zone out the couch potato needs the aid of what we call a television set with its bright lights, ever-changing images and various levels of sound to help them carry out a sloth-like existence.

 * Telemarketers – Without question, these are much-maligned folks. Collectively, they are among everyone's favorite

verbal punching bags. I confess, from time to time even I take a verbal swipe at them much to the amusement of myself and others that might be with me at the time I put forth a zinger or two. Nevertheless, they deserve an appreciation from us, too. So many of us live fast-paced lives in which we are often rushing from one commitment to another: classes, a second job, soccer practice, drinks with the boys at Hooters, etc. Consequently, family units often have the dual challenge of spending time together or even keeping track of what time it is during the course of a day. This, then, leads me to the debt of gratitude we owe telemarketers. Their non-stop calls serve as a reminder it is dinner time. If we are not eating dinner when they call, then we should be.

* Power Naps – I know. I know. A power nap is more of a thing rather than a living, breathing being. I still want to give them an appreciation because they make us feel good about ourselves. Taking a regular nap, for instance, makes us sound as if we are being lazy and non-productive. But a "power nap" sounds so powerful and strong. Sure, even though we are still sawing wood, it sounds as if at the same time we are also mowing the yard or balancing our checkbook. But just between you and me, I think I will stick with regular naps. Power naps are too much work.

* Tailgaters. We are driving along the highway going about fifty to sixty miles per hour and the driver behind us seems practically in our backseat. How annoying. How aggravating. Yet how refreshing. I say that because this idiot is finally giving us something legitimate to fume about and that we can actually correct. We can slow down until the person passes us. Another viable strategy to get them off our tail is to pull over into another lane. Those two measures serve as a nice balance to just screaming profanities at that driver.

* Return Addresses – The mail comes so we take it out of the mail box and start leafing through everything: a bill, some junk mail, another bill, another bill, more junk mail, and, oh, what's this? It appears to be a letter. But quickly after making that great revelation, you look at the return address and the mystery of this unexpected piece of mail is quickly solved. You know it is either a letter from an uncle with whom you have not talked in over ten years, another piece of junk mail cleverly disguised as a letter, or a note from your insurance agent wishing you a happy (fill-in-the-blank). There is enough in life that most of us struggle with as it is. This is why return addresses deserve an appreciation: they solve mysteries and therefore are not part of that list.

* Chameleons – This one is personal to me. I had a pet chameleon once. While I cannot say it was among my favorite pets, I will concede it was among the most intriguing. I hardly ever saw the damn thing move. I remember sitting in front of its tank for what seemed liked hours waiting for it to do something – anything – but it never did. Then, my mother would call me from downstairs and I would turn to respond. Literally, seconds later when I turned back to the tank I would see the chameleon was now on the other side of the tank in a different position. I found this to be both incredibly frustrating, exciting and ultimately unsatisfying (not unlike a girl I used to date in high school). Looking back, I would say this pet taught me the importance of patience but that being patient does not always lead to a pleasing result. Postscript: My pet chameleon did not live a long time. As is the case with goldfish and parakeets, you really have no way of knowing they are close to death's door. They seem normal and

then suddenly they are dead. One thing I will say on behalf of other creatures, such as dogs and cats and even people, at least when they are not feeling well and are about to go to their final reward everyone around them knows it. But that was definitely not the case with my chameleon. In fact, because it spent so much of its time not moving, I suspect the thing had been dead for days before I finally figured out it was, in fact, dead. When living in capacity, maybe chameleons should think about that.

* Nature Sound Effects Machines – I am not one who likes to sleep outdoors. I love the outdoors and love being out in nature, but when it comes time to call it a day and turn in, give me the comfort of a nice bed, clean sheets, shower, etc. any and every time. One great thing about my cousin who I go on hiking adventures with every year is that he, too, is not a fan of sleeping outdoors. The fact we share the same preference makes our trips all the more enjoyable. (For instance, how many people can say one day they hiked the Grand Canyon and the next spent the night at the Bellagio in Las Vegas?) Having said that, I do appreciate there are those who do like camping out and who might actually consider people like my cousin and I to be wussies. For those of you who do, I can assure you that you will get no argument from either my cousin or me.

More and more, I am noticing what I call nature sound effect machines that people keep next to their beds. The little box contains an array of nature sounds that range from whales and the rain forest to thunderstorms and heavy winds. Whenever I find one at a hotel or bed & breakfast place at which I may be staying I make great use of them. They are fun to listen to and do, in fact, help make drifting off to sleep a bit easier. For me, it provides some of the more pleasant sounds of nature without some of the more unpleasant realties of nature. So, here's a big thank-you to those magic boxes.

* Flip Flops. Some people give them the fancy name of sandals. Whenever I am in the company of fancy people or, as Cole Porter might refer to them, "swells," I say "sandals". But the truth is they are and forever will be flip flops. At least to me. These pseudo shoes represent the best of both worlds: they help give us the sensation of walking around in our bare feet yet the security of knowing that we really aren't. The only problem I personally have with them is their noise. I like their name but have trouble with their constant "flip" and "flop" that is as unrelenting as a leaky faucet or a stuck car horn. Come to think of it, perhaps one big difference between flip flops and sandals is the noise. Maybe I'll start wearing sandals.

* Small Talk. Anyone who denies participating in small talk is stretching the truth. They may not enjoy it. They may do their best to avoid it. But they and the rest of us do it and that's all there is to it. Sure, small talk can seem like a waste of time. Still, given the bad rap it receives, it is about time somebody stuck up for small talk and said a few words on its behalf. Let me begin by saying most of us are not Noel Coward or Dorothy Parker or, more recently, Jon Stewart or Jerry Seinfeld when it comes to conversation and banter. Most of us are not naturally witty, nor do we always have a string a clever comments at the ready just waiting to be launched like mini drone missiles. We find ourselves in a conversation with someone we either do not know or know very well but we feel a sense of trying to make the best of what often is an awkward moment. Yes, it is a challenge but it is small talk that helps see us through.

The weather, family, work, the local sports team and traffic are among the key topics that dominate any small talk conversation. Each one is a bulls-eye when it comes to taking up time, creating an illusion of meaningful interaction, and buying each participant time until they figure out a way to remove themselves from this scene. However, there is risk in this and people need to know it. There is always a chance – a slight one but still a chance – that the person you are talking with, but do not want to be, will actually say something of interest. For instance, the interaction could be crawling along perfectly. You feel you have put in a polite amount of time and are about to say, "Well, Fred, it's been great seeing you but I need to run," when Fred says something like, "Yeah, the weather hasn't been the same since that UFO landed in my backyard." Now what? You were poised to leave when Fred drops this bombshell. While you are still not any more interested in him, to not ask about what he just said either makes you look like a jerk or exposes the fact you were only barely listening to anything he was saying. (One of the unspoken rules of small talk is that each party has to pretend to be genuinely engaged in the conversation.) If it was a chess match, one could say Fred just trapped your queen. At this point, you have little choice but to say, "UFO! What happened?"

Once you ask a question that open-ended, you, of course, have just taken a big step further into dear Fred's web. Your only hope is that Fred's UFO story really does turn out to be interesting. If not, then the sad truth is you are now involved in more mindless chatter until you can regain your footing and initiate the escape line you were about to use until Fred crossed you up. No question, this is a dance not much different to the one between a mongoose and a cobra, except you and probably the other person, too, are looking for a way out. All this is to say I believe we need to give a shout-out to small talk. It helps us navigate those situations in which we are expected to be polite and talk but do not want to.

 * Restaurant Buzzers – There is a fairly recent innovation in restaurants that I like. It is the device patrons are given when they are unable to be seated right away. These square-shaped devices light up and vibrate when one's table is ready. Who among us does not feel a surge of genuine joy the moment that little contraption starts shaking in our hand? It is a great feeling not all that different from hearing your name called at the reading of a deceased relative's will. You know a goody is about to follow.

 This is why I think all prisoners who find themselves on death row should be given one of these devices. Being on death row, of course, is the worst of the worst. You are biding your time until it is time for your execution. All joking aside, that has got to be awful. This brings me back to the restaurant buzzer. It is my contention that this clever device has just as much of a direct impact on people as did the bell on Pavlov's dog. The difference is, instead of us salivating as was the case of the dog, it, in essence, triggers a feeling of joy within our system. Though the feeling may last only a few moments, it is still one that is all-positive. By issuing these buzzers to prisons on death row, we would be giving them a similar thrill in their darkest hour. Of course, as it is with restaurants, the prison would have to return the device on the way to his or her "table".

Teaching

I must say there are several professions that come under the category of "noble". Teaching is one of them. Others include police officer, fire fighter, public servant and anyone in the military. Then there are those that fall a bit below those top tier callings even though they do possess a level of importance. These range from the person who is the first clown assigned to get into the clown car and the sound guy for any mariachi band, to the food taster for any evil dictator and the person who turns the music sheet for the classic pianist during a recital. Yes, they serve a purpose but – let's be honest – those poor souls have a job that most of us look at and think, "Thank God that's not me."

But teachers are a special breed no matter the level at which they teach. Throughout this, uh, book I have alluded to the fact that I have taught for many years. I still do. But in no way do I view whatever abilities I might have to be anything beyond average at best. In fact, the best part of my classes is the students. They make it all sing. I am not sure I do. Still, the profession is vital to the survival and well-being of any society. I am lucky to be a small part of it. Okay. That's enough of the mushy talk about that. The truth is, who would you rather run into on a hot spring or summer day: a teacher or the guy behind the counter in a Mister Softee truck? (Author's note: I want any reader that answered "teacher" to put down this book and walk away. You are no longer invited to keep reading.) That is not necessarily a put-down of teachers. Even on a cold winter day, the Mister Softee guy would be hard to top.

One of my first teaching experiences was at a men's prison. No, I was not an inmate trying to get my sentence reduced. At the time, I worked at a community college and, as a way of making a few extra bucks, became part of a program it had with the local correctional institute. For it, I put together an introductory journalism class. I figured that might be a tad more acceptable to the authorities than a class in tunnel-digging, pole vaulting or hostage-taking. Fortunately, it was. Speaking of hostage-taking, I confess I did think about the possibility of being grabbed by one or several of the inmates and being used as a bargaining chip for their release. I shared my concern with the director who assured me without hesitation, "Oh we're not worrying about that." As an aside, I think it was at that moment I got a glimpse of the value the community college placed on me. I suspect if something like that had ever happened, then right now I would either be dead or a very used sex-toy for cellblock number two.

The truth is, I found the inmates to be very well behaved and cordial. This class and others made available to them were designed to give each prisoner an opportunity to demonstrate their commitment to rehabilitation. One inmate, I recall, used to sit in the back of our designated area with his arms folded and eyes closed. After one of our classes, he came up and assured me he was not sleeping. "This is how I listen," he said. I, of course, was not about to challenge him. It would not have mattered to me if he sat in the back and played Hungry Hippo. Still, it was nice of him to tell me. To say the least, for that class I was a very easy grader. While I cannot remember exactly how many inmates were in my class, I do recall several dropping out over the duration of our time together. It was not because they were released or escaped. It seems a couple of them had been severely injured in prison fights and were either hospitalized, had their class privileges revoked, or both.

I did not give them any tests or homework. Whatever work they did, I had them do during our class. Actually, I considered giving homework but then I got to thinking: what would be my punishment if they missed a homework assignment? I couldn't have them stay after school, nor would I have them come to my office so I could give them a stern talking to. My goal, in the words of the late Rodney King, was to "get along" and perhaps share some information with them they might find useful.

Going into the class I was warned that some of the inmates may try to see how they could communicate with me outside the class. If they do, I was told to politely thank them and have them contact the community college. A few did, claiming they needed help reaching a friend or relative. I followed the advice of the prison authorities and had no problems in that regard. In my limited experience, I never came across anyone I would consider to be a criminal mastermind. Rather, these were guys who had done bad things – a few in particular were in prison for being convicted of very violent acts – and were paying the price for their wrongdoings. Overall, at least to me, they seemed nice enough.

Other than that year in this program, all my teaching has been at a college level and outside of prison. Each time I stand in front of a class of students, I am nervous that I will be found out as I am not as well-versed in the topic as I should be. Fortunately, that has not yet happened though it seems like it is just a matter of time before it does. The good news is that I am prepared. For instance, if a student asks me to explain the difference between a crock pot and a wok, my first reaction would be to give him or her the same look the family dog would if you handed him a telephone and said, "Here boy, it's for you." Following that, I would do one of two things: call a fire drill or faint. Either strategy is fool-proof. The fire drill would require everyone to evacuate the room and even the building. Fainting, on the other hand, would be trickier. It would force me to pretend I am unconscious until everyone finally left the room. As this could take a while, it would be important for me to land on the floor in a position that is comfortable, yet not obviously so. As I write this, I am thinking I should practice that here at home until I get really good at it. A fake faint is one of those things one has to get right the first time. It is like french-kissing a garbage disposal: you do not want to have to do it twice.

When it comes to being recognized by students, there are some teachers who insist upon being called by their title (professor or doctor, for example) or, if they are neither, then by Mister or Ms. (last name). That kind of formality has never been important to me. Consequently, I have had students call me by title, by Mister or even by just my first or last name. It is all good. Anything else, however, would not be acceptable. For instance, I would not wish to be called "the Georgia Peach", "Santa's little helper", "Mister Wiggly", "Miss Daisy", "Vlad the Impaler" or "the hardest working man in show business". Besides the fact all those tags have been taken, none of them hold true to me. (May I add that I am especially glad none of the inmates I taught wanted to call me either "Mister Wiggly" or "Miss Daisy".) While I do not mind a certain level of informality between teacher and student, I do insist certain lines should not be crossed. For example, I would never allow any student to give me a dutch rub, a wedgie, play "got your nose" with me, or pull my finger. Talk about a slippery slope. If I were to do any of those things, there is a slight chance it would compromise my authority. Further, if a student were to ask me to, say, shave my head, go streaking with them, or open up a joint account in an off shore bank, then I would say no to those things as well. After all, one has to maintain a certain level of professional dignity that others must recognize and respect.

One of my big challenges as a teacher revolves around giving them their final grade at the conclusion of a semester. Usually, semesters are fifteen to sixteen weeks in length. Over such a period of time I have usually established some level of connection with a student. This does not necessarily mean we have become BFFs, but it does suggest we have developed some level of rapport. This might mean the student and I enjoy laughing at the same type of people, we both regret there were not more books in the "Twilight" series, or both of us give thanks to be living in a country where people are free to wear baseball caps backwards or, better yet, sideways.

Given such a bond, I hate it when I have to give a student a bad grade. Good grades, such as an A or B, are easy, as you might expect. When there is a connection with a student, doing something that makes them happy is a nice feeling. But then there is the matter of bad or – worst of all – failing grades. I only fail a student if I feel I have no other choice. For instance, if a masked gunman were to order me to fail a student, then I would.

(Sorry, but that's the way I roll.) Another scenario is if a student fails to take the final exam or hand in any of their major assignments. Even given that, however, I still hesitate before lowering the boom. I think I would make a terrible executioner. The condemned has just placed their head onto the chopping block. I am standing over them with the ax raised and all the while I am thinking, "Boy, would I rather be somewhere else... What can I do to get out of this? I know. I'll use the old 'I lost my contact lens' trick. Better yet. I'll call a fire drill or do the old fake faint routine. It's a good thing I have been practicing that at home." At this point, of course, the condemned would be squirming around. Perhaps they might even look up at me with a "what the hell is going on?" expression on their face. I would try to avoid making direct eye contact with them as I often do with students I am about to fail. What eases the discomfort of it all – at least in my experience – are that the few students I have failed have not been surprised by my final verdict.

In keeping with this is the matter of providing students with intelligent, useful and timely feedback. I struggle with each of these. On occasion, a student will hand in something that is so striking that the feedback I want to give them is to go out and buy as many lottery tickets as possible and hope for the best. On the other end of the spectrum, sometimes a student will produce work that is extremely stimulating and provocative as anything I could hope for. No matter the quality of their work, however, all students need to be encouraged. Hell, we all do. Whenever I find myself in an elementary school setting, I am struck by how much effort the teacher makes to recognize effort and how much pleasure the little boy or girl receives from those special pats on the back. I do not believe that thrill we feel whenever we do something well and are recognized for it ever goes away. I certainly see it at the college level. Being in a position of power, as teachers are, provides them with a unique opportunity to lift up or tear down. This is true of bosses, too. I have had a boss or two in my lifetime who took full advantage of that kind of power, particularly in a negative way. It is no fun to watch and even painful to see the impact such meanness can and does have on another person. No matter the form in which it takes, power is a dangerous thing to give anyone. Teachers can and do make such a monumental difference with this power at their disposal. I sometimes wonder if education programs that train teachers spend enough time helping these men and women truly appreciate the importance of using their power over others.

The other aspect about teaching I find to be particularly challenging is coming up with enough to talk about for the hour or so I am with a class. That can be a long time to hold anyone's attention. In fact, every time I walk out in front of a class, I find myself more and more appreciating Weird Al Yankovich or that earlier comedic trailblazer Rip Taylor. Even though I know mentioning those two here is laughably obvious, I recognize there may be a few readers who do not see how Weird Al and Rip fit into this at all. So, with apologies to the great majority of you, let me take a few moments to bring those few up to speed. We live in a world of great and non-stop activity and an unbelievable amount of diversion. Further, due in large measure to the advanced technology now at our disposal, the information we are called upon to process, interpret, judge and ultimately act on is unrelenting. Additionally, as this applies to students, if one throws into the mix their need to obtain and hold onto jobs, their understandable desire to socialize and have fun (damn them), and the realty of paying bills, coping with their own family matters, and the usual array of unexpected challenges life throws at all of us, including flat tires, allergies, out of town company, and oversleeping, then it is plain they have much to contend with during the course of a routine day and week.

Mentioning all this is not meant to make excuses for students or explain away any missteps they may or may not make. After all, we so-called grown-ups have to deal with this stuff, too. (But the reality is, those of us who have been dealing with "the real world" – however one defines that – longer than most students do not always handle life's challenges all that well either. I only mention that to note that we and they have a lot more in common than we may want to admit.) Fair or not, much goes on in the lives of students that teachers have to compete with whether it is for a one-hour class or an entire semester. Consequently, it is no longer enough for teachers to be experts in their field of study or extremely knowledgeable in the topic or topics they teach. Those days are gone. Not only do teachers need to be solid communicators but their style of communicating must be one that engages students, holds their attention, and, dare I say it, even goes as far as to entertain them. This, then, brings me back to Weird Al and Rip.

If the comedic style of those two guys could be captured in one word, then that word would be "outrageous". Whether it was smashing fruit, squirting seltzer water at the audience or spinning their toupee around on their head, those guys would do anything for a laugh (not quite as much as Dick Cheney, but close). Even though not everything they did was funny, without question it was captivating and, more to the point, attention-getting and attention-keeping. While on stage, the eyes of the audience rarely stray from them. This is why I think of those two every time I step in front of a class full of students. I may know my stuff but I need to present it in a way that is both engaging and interesting. Otherwise, I will lose them to all those other parts of life, including their i-phones, other classes that may be as interesting as I want mine to be, or even to each other.

In case you are wondering, no, I have never squirted seltzer water at the class or knocked watermelons at them with a baseball bat – yet – but in my own way, and in keeping within my own comfort level, I strive to be both entertaining and informative; entertaining not necessarily just for the sake of eliciting yuks from the class, but rather to better serve the information I am seeking to impart. How well I do and have done all these years I will leave to others to say, but the fact is sometimes I do better than others and always I try to be better than I was the day before. Teaching, much like the world that all of us share, is a constant challenge designed to make all of us – teacher and student – as wise and competent as we hope to be.

Under My Skin

One of the all-time great songs is Cole Porter's "I've Got You Under My Skin." There have been numerous versions and interpretations of this classic. To me, they are all good simply on the basis of the strength of the song itself. Looking at this world of ours, there are definitely a number of things that are under my skin, some in a good way and some not. Some may judge my choices to be trivial. I also recognize they may be unique to me. Nevertheless, the following are things I find to be annoying. And since I am such a sharing guy, I would like to share a few of them with you.

 Bugs. One thing that bugs me is bugs. I am not a fan. Thus, it is too bad for me as scientists estimate there are over one million different kinds of insects in the world. Taking this a bit further, it is also estimated there are over two hundred million insects to every single human being. It occurs to me there are probably a ton of these critters staring at me right now as I write this. I wonder what they are saying about me? Don't snicker. I do not believe for a moment they are not whispering little asides about me to each other. If I and a bunch of my friends were tiny in size and in the same room as, say, a giant rhino, you can bet we would be talking about it. And, knowing me and some of my friends, it is likely our comments would not be all that flattering either.

Those insects that are not talking about me are no doubt engrossed in doing something. To them, it is probably constructive. Maybe they are building a little recreation room, a homeless shelter, a shopping mall, a microscopic Starbucks, or a nursery. Whatever they are up to, I am pretty sure I do not like it. For one thing, this is my room, not there's. If they are so darn enterprising, then it seems like if they wanted to they could or should be able to communicate what they are proposing to do, so we could discuss it. I like to think of myself as being open-minded. Maybe I would go along with what they want to do. But the least they could do is ask rather than just plow ahead. It is rude. What is the point of my being at the top of the food chain if those below me are not going to ask my permission to do something?

Blue Tooth. One of the things I have resolved never to do is wear and use a blue tooth. I should qualify this before going too far down this road. Mainly, I am talking about those little contraptions one attaches to one of one's ears so they can receive in-coming phone calls immediately. The other kind of headphones are okay, though I generally shy away from them, too. First of all, I would hate anything attached to one ear while nothing is attached to the other. It would be like wearing one sock. Not only would that not look cool, but it would be uncomfortable. Related to this are drivers who have speaker phones in their cars. Certainly, I do not believe people should text and drive, especially if they drive a rickshaw. (Is it just me, or are rickshaw drivers never arrested for drunken driving? How do they get away with it?) You see them driving along the highway with both hands on the steering wheel and they are talking, laughing, etc. Assuming they actually are talking on their speaker phone, at the same time to other drivers they look to be insane. I find this a bit disconcerting. It makes me want to move at least two lanes away from them.

Talking During a Movie. Most, if not all of us, are fans of James Bond movies. It is always fun when a new 007 movie is released. Even watching them – or some of them – a second or third time is enjoyable, too. Whenever the Bond movies come up in conversation, someone always wonders what their life would be like if they had a license to kill. If I had such a license, how often would I use it? It is hard to say, of course, though there would be moments of genuine temptation. People who talk during movies would definitely be up for debate. But in all seriousness, I would not be comfortable with having that kind of power. I definitely do not want to kill anyone. I would much prefer having a license to annoy. To be able to really annoy the hell out of someone without fear of retribution or punishment would be great. My method would not be ordinary by any stretch. I would tell my victims they were included in a will of a fabulously rich person who just died. I would have them show up while the so-called will is being read and then talk throughout the entire reading. You can bet this would annoy them greatly.

This may seem a tad too harsh, but it occurs to me that if we can put a man on the moon, then that means we can put people who talk during movies on the moon, too.

Illegal Parkers. All of us have been to shopping malls and, at times, found it difficult to find a parking space. Suddenly we see one and a great sense of relief washes over us. That feeling is dashed when we notice the car is actually taking up two spaces, thus making it impossible for us and anyone else to take advantage of what otherwise would be an adequate space. People who park illegally, particularly in this way, have a very secure spot under my skin. In terms of what to do about them, see "talking during a movie." Perhaps these crackerjack road warriors can drive the space ship.

Too Much Honesty. There are those who profess to be completely honest. This is their conclusion because they say they believe in "telling it like it is". Whatever. If I go to the trouble of picking out an outfit that I think makes me look sharp, I do not want some so-called friend telling me – without being asked – that I look anything but that. My ego is fragile enough as it is. If someone is going to be brutally honest, then I want some time to prepare; perhaps to go find some cotton I can stuff in my ears first. Related to this are those who have an opinion about anything and everything. It is as if they are everyone's self-appointed critic.

The Designated Hitter Rule. I am a baseball traditionalist. It was a dark day when teams were allowed to insert specialized hitters into the lineup and relieve the pitcher from having to swing a bat at all. A player on the field not having to hit is like having a lullaby without a drum solo. It is not natural. Perhaps a better analogy is that it is like a Dr. Seuss book without any rhymes. Pitchers should be made to pick up a bat and swing it like everyone else. When did it become acceptable for them to be inept at the plate? Not only is everyone else on the field expected to catch and throw with great precision, but they are expected to hit well, too. Let's get with it, pitchers. Even though the designated hitter rule has been in effect since 1973, I see no reason why it cannot and should not be revoked.

Speaking of baseball, growing up I used to spend an enormous amount of time pouring over the statistics of old time baseball players and reading about their lives. I mention this as I want to pass along two pieces of wisdom to any reader considering a career as a major leaguer. The first nugget is inspired by one of the original members of the St. Louis Cardinal's Gashouse Gang. I speak of Pepper Martin. Born in Temple, Oklahoma, Pepper played from 1928 to 1944. He retired with lifetime batting average of .298 and a reputation for being a fierce competitor with his headfirst slides into most any base he was attempting to steal or take. Perhaps because of rural upbringing, he was also known for not wearing any underwear or protection under his uniform. Ouch. So, my first piece of advice to any would-be players is to not do what Pepper did. You may not be a fan of underpants, but slap on a jockstrap at least.

The second nugget is not as nuanced as the first. To be a professional baseball player you must have a lot of talent. If you do not have this necessary ingredient, then you are not going to make it to the big leagues. I found this out firsthand. But in fairness to me, this is an easy mistake to make. After all, I pitched several no-hitters in little league and even managed to clobber a few home runs. Given that, taking the field at Fenway Park or Yankee Stadium seemed a foregone conclusion. To put it mildly, that scenario never came to pass. However, I am glad to report I have attended games at those and other stadiums and had a ton of fun each and every time.

Convertibles. I understand lots of people like driving with the top down, especially in the middle of the summer. Also, convertibles do look cool and sporty and make any of their drivers look snazzy. Fortunately, there are other ways to look snazzy without having to drive a car without the top. Wearing a nice looking scarf is one way. My primary objection to convertibles is that I do not find them to be all that practical. You cannot leave important papers in the front or backseat as they will soon end up decorating the nearest highway. Then there is the matter of leaving the car parked somewhere while you go run errands. Depending upon where you are, who knows what kind of shape the interior will be when you return? Finally, and this is a big one, these cars are seasonal. Winter and rain are their particular kryptonite. Hard-top cars may not be invulnerable, but at least they can be driven all year round.

Breakfast in bed. This is one of those concepts that sounds a lot better than it really is. Talk about impracticality. To my way of thinking, it is way too much of a logistical challenge to balance a tray of silverware, plate of breakfast food, juice or coffee, etc. on your lap to make this gesture anything close to pleasant. I recognize that some see serving their loved one breakfast in bed as a big romantic gesture. Not me. I may be smiling on the outside, but inside I am thinking I would so much rather be sitting at the breakfast table and reading the morning paper than endure trying to eat while not spilling anything on the bed sheets. Besides, I can't even eat some cookies in bed without getting crumbs all over the sheets. Chowing down on breakfast with the eggs, toast, jelly, etc. is way out of my league. All that aside, I wonder why no one ever tried lunch or dinner in bed? Maybe it was felt that either one of these meals would be far too much trouble. Why is it believed breakfast would be any different?

Public Proposals. Several times over the years I have been at sports events in a public arena when, during halftime or a break in the action, we look up at the jumbo screen and see a young couple. The guy turns to the girl, strings together a few sentences about eternal love, being very happy and growing old together and then asks for her hand in marriage. The girl, of course, is shocked and embarrassed. But, from the ones I have personally witnessed, rallies enough to kiss that big lug of hers and accept his proposal. The two kiss, all the fans in the audience cheer, and some type of celebratory music blasts out over the loud speakers. Now can we get back to the game?

This so-called romantic scenario bugs me on a number of levels. Having said that, I would love it if one time one of these girls would say, "Uh, listen Clark. Thanks. You're a nice guy and all but no I don't want to marry you. Are you kidding? Besides, I'm banging your brother. Now could you get me those chicken wings like I asked?"

I recognize our friend Clark and the multitude of other young men in love who have tried this stunt may defend their actions by claiming it to be a highly romantic gesture. But the fact is, it is a highly selfish one, too. By proposing marriage in front of thousands of people, or millions if you do it on television as some have, you are putting a ton of pressure on your lady friend. Under that kind spotlight, who among us would not say "yes" just to get off the jumbo screen? I might even be inclined to accept Clark's proposal at that point. (But rest assured, while wolfing down the chicken wings I would let him know I didn't mean it.) I do not see proposing marriage as a spectator sport any more than I see conceiving a child or completing joint tax returns. These are all private moments that should be left that way.

Smoking While Driving. I do not see this as often as I used to, but unfortunately there will be times when I am driving along and I see a fellow driver flick a cigarette out the window of their car. This, as much as anything, gets under my skin. I can only hope there is a special hell for people who do that. I wish cigarette manufacturers would somehow build a boomerang element into each cigarette so when the smoker tosses his or her "cig" out the car window it would bounce right back to them. And if their car windows were closed, then the discarded cigarette would have the capability of following them home. Littering is bad enough as it is. To my mind, smoking gives it a run for its money. Still, if a guy or gal wants to light up one, then fine. But, like marriage proposals, to all you smokers out there, keep it to yourself.

Duck Hunters. It is not my intent to criticize those who hunt. Many, without question, are good people. While it is not for me, I do not begrudge those who find pleasure in hunting down deer, quail or other game. Having said that, on the social scale of hunters I have to think those who hunt duck have to be at or near the lowest rung of the ladder. Think about it. The people who do this go to a ton of trouble – put on hunter's gear, get up in the wee hours of the morning, often taking a bird dog with them, use duck calls and decoys, and hide in duck blinds – all to shoot and kill a bird that most children could lure in with a bag of bread. Wave that bread around and any duck will either swim or waddle up to within inches of you. At that range, you would not even have to waste a bullet. A simple mallet would do.

If someone wants to impress as a hunter, then go into the woods with nothing but a spoon, slingshot and a tin of Altoids and see if you can take down a rhino.

Never Do This

If nothing else, we all live in a world of dos and don'ts. These rules, regulations, decrees, laws or whatever one wants to call them give us the parameters around which we can and should conduct ourselves. For instance, we know we should never try to high-five the Queen Mother or rub noses with any animal with teeth and foam coming out of its mouth. Those aside, drawing from my experience and years of accumulated wisdom, I wish to share a few more guidelines with you that, collectively, may not guarantee a winning lottery ticket, a greater love life or front row seats at next year's Academy Awards, but they may help you avoid, at the minimum, embarrassment or, at the worst, getting the shit kicked out of you. (*Author's note: These are in no particular order.*)

1. Never tell an Alzheimer's patient to "Hold that thought."

2. Honeymooners: The wife should never point and giggle when her newlywed husband is naked. The man should not bring along hand puppets. Yes, they are cute and everyone loves them. But they will not enhance your performance, nor will they put your wife in the mood any quicker than champagne, strawberries or Barry White.

3. Do not walk into a liquor or convenience store with a ski mask pulled over your face. Even if you have no intention of robbing the place, you are leaving yourself open to being widely misinterpreted. On the other hand, however, you probably will be given faster service.

4. Never laugh out loud at a funeral home. Even if you are having a good time and are swapping dirty jokes with long-lost relatives and friends, it is important you at least give the appearance of being somber and having respect for the deceased, even if you never liked them and they still owed you money at the time they "kicked off".

5. Never bring a fax machine to the movies. If you think people talking on a cell phone during a movie is annoying, then you can imagine how aggravating it is if someone starts faxing papers right after the opening credits. Save the faxing for when you are in the car driving home.

6. Never play "Simon Says" with any one named Simon. It's a tough enough game as it is. The last thing you want is to make your opponent feel cocky.

7. For anyone in prison, even if you have had a rough day in the yard or the shower, never tell your cellmate, "Boy, I sure could use a hug."

8. Just because they are beautiful and run fast, never assume deer don't have their clumsy moments just like the rest of us. In fact, I bet somewhere a deer is bumping its head on a tree branch right now.

9. If your boss makes an ass of themselves in front of a room full of people, do not join in with everyone else and laugh. Wait till they leave the room and then talk about what they just did

behind their back. That way, if it ever gets back to them, you can always deny it.

10. I know others have said this before, but it bears repeating: never wear the combination of short pants, white socks and sandals. Shame on you if you have to ask why.

One More Cat Story

Sometimes when I get together with my girlfriends, we talk about relationships. Usually it is about the ones we have with our husbands but sometimes it is about marriage in general. We all agree that we are glad we have them and how lucky we are to have husbands who give us such great support. I know I try to support my husband and be very understanding about how much going down to the dockyards relaxes him and seems to make him less grumpy. He never really tells me about what he does down there but that's okay 'cause I know he always comes back in a good mood. He sometimes calls it his "special place".

But I have my own special place and that's when I am cuddling with Mister Purr. He gives me all the attention I need. I'm sure if he could we talk, then he would love hearing about my sewing and collection of spittoons. Right now, I have over seventy of them. No one I know can believe I have so many. That's why I feel so proud of it. I can't even think of one person who comes even close to having that many. But as close as Mister Purr and I are, I know our relationship has not always been smooth sailing. There was a time when Mister Purr actually disappeared for nearly a year. What a terrible time that was for me!

At first, I thought Mister Purr had gone outside and gotten lost. I refused to believe he had run away from our home. "Why would he do that?" I kept asking everyone. "We were so happy together." Every morning I would make him a bowl of hot milk. I call it his hot cocoa. What other cat had such a nice treat every day? Yet one day I woke to find Mister Purr gone. I couldn't believe it. I was so frantic and worried. At first I must have gone around the neighborhood five or six times a day looking for him... calling out his name... looking for signs of my Mister Purr. Even my husband was puzzled. He even tried to reassure me by suggesting Mister Purr may have gotten outside and been attacked by a pack of dogs; possibly ripped to shreds and eaten by them, he said. But that didn't help. The thought of Mister Purr in the outside weather without my favorite sweater I had sewn for him was almost too much for me to bear.

Months and months passed and still no Mister Purr. I never gave up hope, yet I confess to wondering if I would ever see him again. Then, one day – it was a Wednesday – there was a knock on the door and within moments everything was all right again. Mister Purr was home. There were several agents from the FBI at the door. One of them had a carrier-on box and inside it was Mister Purr. He looked healthy and fit and I wanted to give him a giant hug. Mister Purr looked good, too. The agent stepped inside our house, set down the carrier, opened it and out popped Mister Purr. I remember I actually squealed when I saw my favorite fuzzy thing.

Having Mister Purr back after being gone so long caused a lot of commotion, of course. But, finally, we and the agents sat down. They explained, as best as they were able, where Mister Purr had been and what he had been doing all this time. It is still a really amazing story. The agents explained that in our city an illegal drug running operation had been operating. Millions of dollar of drugs were being laundered under the noses of the police and nothing was being done to stop it. Federal authorities needed someone to infiltrate the gang, get inside the operation, and collect enough evidence so arrests could be made and it could be stopped.

"None of us could get that deep inside 'cause they all knew all of us. We needed a fresh face. Someone they would never suspect," explained one of the agents. "Then we thought of Mister Purr. After what he did with those terrorists on the plane, we felt he would be a natural."

"That's right," a second agent chimed in. "A cat would be the last thing the drug lords would suspect. The cat could pretend to be a stray and start showing up at the drug lord's house. Purring and meowing as if all he wanted was a warm house, some food and to have his tummy rubbed. We felt Mister Purr would be perfect. Obviously, we knew he was resourceful and had nerves of steel.

"We knew how good he was when surprise was on his side," the agent continued. "But did Mister Purr have the guile to pull this off? Would he be willing to put his life on the line like this? If those killers ever found out he was not a simple stray cat but an actual agent working for us, then he would be on his own. We would be forced to disavow any knowledge of him and he, in all likelihood, would be killed."

Fortunately, Mister Purr agreed to take on this dangerous mission even though it meant going undercover, risking his life and leaving me for how long no one really knew. Mister Purr also knew he could not share with me what he was about to do because that would put my life and my husband's in danger. So, one day Mister Purr disappeared. Just like that. I can see now how brave he was.

I wanted to hear all the details about what had happened, but the agents explained they were not at liberty to divulge any secrets. We did not have the kind of security clearance apparently one needs to be given that kind of information. But they said we would have been very proud of our kitty. I remember one of the agents said with a kind of chuckle, "It is one of those things, if this had been a movie or even a story in some silly joke book, one would laugh it off as being too unbelievable to be true."

I had to laugh at that, too. The thought of my cat infiltrating the lair of a drug cartel and collecting enough evidence to make their arrest possible is hard to believe. I did ask the agents if Mister Purr's life was ever truly in danger at any time. Their response sent chills up and down my back. They never really said "yes," but the fact they hesitated was all I needed to know. At one point, an agent said, Mister Purr's cover was almost blown by one of the drug lord's goldfish. Apparently, Mister Purr and the fish had met before in some past encounter. They said Mister Purr had to take decisive action against the goldfish that resulted in his death; yet Mister Purr was clever enough to make it look like an accident. The fish, they said, was not the only casualty. Mister Purr had to contend with a few of the drug lord's henchmen during some final shoot out. It all sounds so exciting now, but I can only imagine how scary it must have been. Even my husband was impressed.

Those agents spent the whole afternoon at our house. Now I am sitting here with Mister Purr in my lap. I am rubbing his tummy and he is purring like no other kitty in the world. I am so lucky and hope he is never called away on a mission like that ever again.

A Few Quick Shout Outs

Wet Wipes. Anyone who has had a baby and raised them from infancy to adolescence and beyond knows what I am talking about when I say wet wipes have to rank in the top ten of all-time great inventions. Wet wipes are the silver bullet to any mess a child can and does make. A parent without wet wipes is akin to someone being dropped naked in the middle of a major highway and being told to find their way home. However, a parent with wet wipes is like being Superman and being asked to help a kitten down from a tree. Easy-peasy.

Heated Toilet Seats. One of the things all of us have in common is that we use the toilet most, if not each, one of our days. This is nothing for any of us to be ashamed of or have to apologize for. Still, I feel on safe ground predicting it will remain a topic that one is reluctant to bring up in conversation. For instance, in a job interview situation when asked to tell the search committee about themselves, a candidate probably would not volunteer their regular use of a toilet. However, I see a day when this might change. And we can thank the inventors of heated toilets for that. These are five guys who had a vision – and some brains – of taking human kind to a new level of comfort. They are Dave Wilson, Dave Hansen, Anton Kola, Michael Merritt and

John Check. We have heated toilet seats in our house and I must say, not only does it make going to the bathroom any hour of the day or night more pleasurable, but I am now doing a lot more reading than ever before.

Food Samples. I love going into grocery stores that give out sample food treats. In fact, I do not know anyone who does not enjoy that. This is another one of those things that unite us as a people. Depending upon the store, one can come very close to enjoying a full meal from the various food samples that are set out. However, I do feel bad for the folks who prepare and then hand out the free samples. Part of their job is to explain why this particular cut of meat is so tasty and that it is now on sale in aisle four. But no one cares about that. They, like me, just want the free food. As I write this, I have decided I am going to insist upon having lots of food served at my funeral. This way I know there will be large turnout. I just hope that in between bites of coleslaw, ham and jell-o that somebody remembers to bring me up in conversation – at least a little bit.

Little Black Belts. In our neighborhood are several karate and/or judo schools open pretty much to people of all ages. It is not uncommon to walk or drive by any one of them and see young children of elementary school age as well as young and even older adults – not at the same time – in their judo/karate outfits stretching, practicing kicks and throwing each other to the mat. I admire the effort each one of those students of self-defense is making to become proficient at defending themselves in case of attack, or if they need to come to the rescue of an innocent person in trouble.

One thing I like best revolves around the six or seven-year-olds that have worked their way up to a black belt. I take comfort in the knowledge that even though they do, in fact, have a black belt, at my current ripe age I could still take them in a fight. For instance, let us say I am in a restaurant with a friend. We are talking and casually glance around the room and see one of those six-year-old karate masters in uniform with their parents moving toward a nearby table. No big deal. Right? Suddenly, without warning, that karate kid goes rouge. There is immediate chaos. The kid bolts out of the reach of his parents and begins chopping tables, kicking chairs and, with an intense look on his face, dares anyone to stop him. At this point, women in the restaurant are screaming and the men are frozen by fear and uncertainty. That is, every one of them except me. I am cool and stoic in my unshakeable confidence. Others may be feeling panic but not me.

Even though, to the untrained eye, my glance over to that first grader and his parents only moments before may have seemed casual, in reality it was anything but that. In reality, I was taking a full measure of this fighting machine. Despite his impressive, neatly pressed karate uniform and his calm demeanor, as evidenced by the fact he was holding his mother's hand when they followed the hostess to their table, I knew I had this fighting machine's number. I only wish I could explain how I knew other than pure instinct. (Never mind he had been holding a coloring book and crayons in his free hand.) To me, he was a warrior, but one that I knew I could take down if necessary.

This scenario should leave no doubt as to what I say. I am not, by nature, a person who brags about himself or tries to dominate others with my skills and talents. My demeanor is one of quiet confidence. Given all that, yes, I do believe I could take that black belt in karate. This modest, yet pinpoint accurate self-assessment should reassure anyone out in public with me that they are safe if, in our presence, a six-year-old black belt karate master goes rouge. But if, say, an eight-year-old black belt karate master goes rouge, then I think all bets are off.

The Joy of Communicating

If anyone asks you to compile a list of things that are hard to do, then communicating should be near or at the top. Is there anything that comes with more built-in frustration than trying to communicate with another person? I think not.

"Honey, when you go to the store would you pick up some two percent milk?"

"No problem."

Forty-five minutes later the spouse returns. "Here's the milk."

"Wait. This is one percent. I said two."

"Oh. I know you said something about percent but I couldn't remember what."

And so it goes. All of us try to get through our days in one piece, trying to maintain at least a parcel of dignity and avoid as many missteps as possible. But then there is the matter of interacting with others that so often gets in the way. We see speed limit signs that clearly state we should not drive any faster than thirty-five miles per hour. Instead we drive anywhere between five to fifteen miles per hour faster than that even though that is not what the sign or, more importantly, the law is communicating. The recipe calls for two cups of sugar but instead we put in three or four. What's that all about? What's the deal with us? Does our desire to be our own person override the requests or instructions of others? It would seem so.

Then there is the matter of listening. Does anybody really do that any more? I read once that even those who claim to be great listeners use only twenty-five percent of their listening abilities. If those folks are our best, then what does that say about the rest of us? It is like the game of monopoly. Everyone knows what it is. Everyone knows the rules of the game. But have you noticed you never see anyone playing it? Better yet, there is the very popular literary classic, *Robin Hood*. We all know the plot and, of course, are quite familiar with the title character. But how come no one has ever read the damn thing? These communication failures are and forever will be a mystery to me. The same holds true for communication itself.

Earlier, I mentioned that I have taught for many years. For even longer than that I have worked in the communication profession. Specifically, I have worked in the trenches of what we all call public relations. We all know what that is, don't we? Everyone says they do; yet over the past sixty years there have been over five hundred definitions of this term. If everyone knows what it is, then how come so many attempts have been made to define it? We sure do not have that problem with the word "door". Its definition is clear cut, has stood the test of time and has not had to endure any attempts at revision. So, to return to any earlier question, what is the deal with anything related to communication? Is it part of our DNA not to be content with concepts that we cannot reach out and touch? For instance, why can't Hemingway's *The Old Man and the Sea* be about a guy out for a day of fishing? Why can't Herman Melville's *Moby Dick* be simply about a sea captain wanting to kill a whale that bit off his leg?

The funny thing about this – if there is a funny thing about this – is that communication is actually quite simple. One person walks up to another and says, "Shut your trap!" The other person nods and a successful communication exchange has just occurred. What could be more straightforward than that? But suppose the person with the open trap does not want to close it? Suppose they question the other's directive or challenges them to "close it for me"? With that, what was simple takes a different turn. The direct communication exchange has moved to a new level, thus cutting short its initial victory lap. The next thing you know there are raised voices, some pushing, more raised voices, and the next thing you know both parties have pulled out nail guns and have begun turning each other into a dartboard.

My point here is communication is not so simple primarily because it is in our nature to keep it complex, multi-layered and much more of a hit-and-miss proposition. It also helps make life fun and unexpectedly funny. We see and experience all kind of things, some of which communicate a signal that hits the bullseye of our funny bone. For instance, many years ago in college as a reporter for the student newspaper, I was interviewing one of the institution's vice presidents for a story. He was a very serious guy who not only took everything he said seriously, but expected everyone else to do the same as well. Halfway through our time together, he leaned back his chair. Unfortunately, he misjudged the distance between him and the back wall and, sure enough, he toppled backwards over the chair, onto the floor and right smack on his ego. He made me promise not to tell anyone what happened. (Now, about forty years after the fact, I think I am to be commended for not breaking that promise till now.) His backward tumble was unexpected and proved to be a welcome comic bounce to the day. Hopefully, this volume has performed the same function. Sure, miscommunications can be frustrating, but it and the unexpected can also lead to genuine smiles and laughs, if not immediately, then sometime after the fact. On that note, I will close with a little story featuring my same cousin who I have alluded to several times earlier in this book.

One summer day, a bunch of us were playing wiffle ball in my backyard. My cousin and I were on opposing teams. He was their pitcher. I had just been to bat and made it to first base. On the first pitch the next batter hit a blistering line drive right back at my cousin. The liner moved too fast for him to react. The ball hit my cousin square in the Adam's apple. He grabbed his throat and fell backwards to the ground. All of us stood motionless watching my cousin lying on the ground gasping for breath. Sensing my cousin's predicament, I leaped into action. "Run! Run!" I yelled. I and the other runners and batter tore around the bases as the infielders tried to collect themselves. They ran to get the ball that was next to my prone cousin. Several of us scored and I even made it as far as third base. It was a great break in the game for us.

After the play was over, both teams called a timeout to check on my cousin. Fortunately, he was still alive though his teammates were not thrilled with the fact he had given up a few runs at a key moment in the game. For us, it was a double bonus: it put our team back in the lead and gave us all a good laugh. It was one of life's unexpected twists and, for me, a source of pleasant musings.